Standing for

SOCKS

Elissa Brent Weissman

ATHENEUM BOOKS FOR YOUNG READERS

New York · London · Toronto · Sydney

Atheneum Books for Young Readers

An imprint of Simon & Schuster Children's Publishing Division

1230 Avenue of the Americas, New York, New York 10020

Interior illustrations by Jessica Sonkin

Book design by Jessica Sonkin

The text for this book is set in Fairfield LH.

Manufactured in the United States of America

First Edition

2 4 6 8 10 9 7 5 3 1

Library of Congress Cataloging-in-Publication Data

Weissman, Elissa Brent.

Standing for Socks / Elissa Brent Weissman. — 1st ed.

p. cm.

Summary: At the end of fifth grade, Fara decides to wear mismatched socks
as a statement of individuality, but once middle school starts
and she wants to be known for her ideas rather than her clothing,
she feels burdened by an image that she no longer wants.

ISBN-13: 978-1-4169-4801-8

ISBN-10: 1-4169-4801-5

[1. Individuality—Fiction. 2. Middle schools—Fiction.
3. Schools—Fiction. 4. Politics, Practical—Fiction. 5. Socks—Fiction.]

I. Title.

PZ7.W448182St 2009

[Fic]—dc22

2007037215

For Mom and Dad,
whose support has known no match

1. Morning Dew

FARA SAT AT THE KITCHEN TABLE WEARING HER breakfast around her pointer finger like a large, doughy ring. She took a bite of the bagel and then spun it a few inches and took another, eating roundward and inward until there was almost nothing left.

"What an inventive way to eat a bagel," her father said as he put on a pot of coffee.

"Why eat the way everyone else eats?" Fara said. "And it's one less plate to wash," she pointed out, "so we're saving water."

"Original, environmentally conscious, and less work for me. I like the sound of that."

"And it's fun," Fara said as she took the last bite. "You should try it."

"Or maybe I'll think of a new way that tops yours."

"If it has to do with juggling, then that's not fair," Fara said. Mr. Ross often juggled the oranges and bananas from the fruit bowl. Though her mother insisted no one was allowed to juggle fruit, Fara got in more trouble than her dad did when she tried.

"If juggling's not allowed, then I'll need a little more time to think. Is the newspaper here?"

"I'll check. I want to make sure it's warm enough to wear shorts, anyway." Fara ran outside without putting her sneakers on. "Yes!" she said because it was nice and warm outside. "Yuck!" she said because morning dew soaked through her right sock. She balanced so as not to get her left wet as well and picked up the paper from the grass. Back inside, she dropped the paper on the table and poked her father's arm. "I wet my right foot getting your newspaper," she said dramatically. She made a fist and raised it in the air. "But I will be okay." Her father sniffled back a fake tear and patted her feet.

Fara went upstairs to her room, scrunching her nose each time the dewy foot hit the stairs. It was not until she'd removed the wet white sock and opened her drawer for a replacement that she realized she was out of white socks. She took out a dark gray pair and pulled one over her right foot. The doorbell rang as she was reaching toward her left foot.

"Fara, Jody's here!" her dad shouted. "Time for school."

Fara and Jody usually met halfway between their houses

to walk to school. Fara checked her watch. Sure enough, she was running late, and she still had to pack her backpack.

"Fars!" her dad called. "Jody!"

Fara dropped the gray sock that was in her hand and hopped off her bed. She threw her books and folder into her backpack, then went downstairs and added her lunch. At the sight of Fara pushing her feet into her sneakers, her father laughed out loud. "One less sock to wash, so we're saving water," he said, giving her a thumbs-up.

Fara tilted her head. Confused but short on time, she kissed him good-bye and ran out the door.

"I love it!" gushed Jody while walking to school. "Are you down to the bottom of your sock drawer?" she guessed.

Fara looked down. One nondewy white sock and one dark gray sock were sticking out of her shoes. So that was what her dad had meant by "one less sock to wash." She laughed; she was saving water. "Well—"

"Oh, I'm dumb," Jody said, shaking her head and making her brown curls fall over her face. "It's because you wanted to match your shirt."

Fara looked at her gray and white Earth Day T-shirt. "Oh, wow," she said. "I didn't even notice that." Her ankles looked funny with the colors alternating as she walked. It was like the gray and white were fighting for precedence, each trying to move ahead of the other.

Jody tucked her hair behind her ears. It fell out again when she jumped in front of Fara to take another guess. "I know. You wanted to make Phillip feel better for that time in second grade when he came to school wearing only one sock by accident."

Fara laughed again. "I forgot about that," she said. "Here." She held out her hand so Jody could take the hair tie she had around her wrist. Fara's straight blond hair was too short to pull into a ponytail, but she always made sure to have a hair tie for Jody.

Jody took the tie and shook Fara's hand in professional thanks. "Oh, I know!"

"It was actually an accident," Fara confessed before Jody could guess again. "My other white sock got wet with morning dew, so I changed it, and then you came and I didn't have time to change the other. But I kind of like it. And it saves water for the wash."

Jody shook her head in amazement. "Even in your accidents you are helping the world. You are the greenest girl on the planet."

Fara beamed. When she and Jody were in second grade, a group called the Green Team came to Harvey Elementary School and did a skit about keeping the earth clean. When they asked who liked to play in the fresh air, lots of kids raised their hands, but Fara raised hers the highest. And when they asked who liked having trees to climb and clean water to drink, Fara clapped and cheered the loudest. And when they had stand everyone who made sure to switch off lights when leaving a room, and who turned off the water while brushing their teeth, and who used recycling bins at home, Fara was the only one who jumped proudly out of her seat every single time. She couldn't believe that all of those things—things she and her parents had been doing ever since she could remember—were not things everyone did. Didn't everyone want fresh air to breathe and tall trees to climb and clean water to drink, like the Green Team said? She wondered if her family did other things that were different. Did other kids go through their toys every birthday and pick one to bring to the Goodwill store? And did other families spend Thanksgiving and Christmas cooking food and serving it to people at a homeless shelter? She didn't know why they wouldn't. But then again, she didn't know why they wouldn't always turn off the water when brushing their teeth, either.

The Green Team gave Fara a green star for living in a green house. Phillip Ronkel shouted out, "But Fara's house is white!" and Melodee Simon jumped up, suddenly remembering that she, too, conserved energy and didn't waste water and recycled. The Green Team ended up giving green stars to everyone who promised to do his or her share to make a difference in the world in any way possible. Most of the class did try for the next few days, but Fara tried the hardest. She even tried starting her own Green Team after lunch that day (called the Green Girls, since only girls showed up to the meeting by the monkey bars), but not even Jody wanted to spend recess picking up trash in the playground. Fara wasn't deterred by the fact that she didn't have a team to help her make a difference, however. And she still wasn't now—she was still trying.

"Well, at least your socks are something new and different," Jody said as the two girls waited to cross the street onto the block where their school was. "Everything has been so *the same* this whole year."

"That's true," Fara agreed. Both she and Jody had Mrs. Ferrara for fifth grade, the same teacher they'd had in fourth grade. While it was great having her best friend in her class two years in a row, it was pretty boring having the same teacher. Mrs. Ferrara liked to follow the same pattern every day and every week, and she assigned the same types of homework and some of the same exact projects as she had last year. She had even come in wearing the same turkey costume on Thanksgiving, and it wasn't nearly as hilarious the second time around. At least Fara had the other fifth-grade teacher, Mrs. Tully, for advanced math, but Jody was in the advanced reading group and the regular math group, both of which were taught by Mrs. Ferrara.

"Mrs. Ferrara keeps saying how next year middle school will be so, so different. It just makes this year seem so, so the same."

"I know," Fara agreed. They stepped onto the sidewalk on the other side of the street. "It'll be fun moving rooms all day. I mean, even if Mrs. Ferrara got moved up to sixth grade, we'd still have six other teachers."

Jody stopped and looked at Fara with wide eyes. "Did you hear that Mrs. Ferrara is moving to sixth grade?" she asked solemnly.

"No, I was just saying. Did you?"

"No."

"Okay," said Fara.

"Okay," said Jody. "Phew."

"How's the last issue of the school newspaper coming?" Fara asked.

Jody raised her eyebrows three times in response. "It's going to be the best one yet," she said. "That's another thing I can't wait for middle school for. The middle school paper comes out every two months, not just twice a year, and there's more to report on, because middle school is a hotbed of activity."

"A hotbed?" Fara asked with a laugh.

"Just wait."

Fara laughed again. "Well, even if it's not a hotbed of activity, at least we only have two more months of the same."

"And your socks are new and different today."

"Yep," said Fara. She grinned. She was happy to bring something new and different to Harvey Elementary School. *Thank you, morning dew,* she thought.

Jody wasn't the only one to notice Fara's socks that day.

"I think you're wearing mismatched socks," Phillip whispered while they did their morning writing assignment.

"Ha! Look!" shouted Ben Huber when Fara got up to sharpen her pencil.

"Cool," said Dana when she sat back down.

Mrs. Tully winked at her during math.

"You definitely stand out," said Jody during lunch. "Everybody's talking about you."

And they were.

"Some people are just hopeless," said Melodee Simon as everyone was leaving at the end of the day. "Like Fara Ross. Did you *see* her *socks* today? *Everybody* knows socks have to match."

Fara looked at her feet. Everybody thought socks *should* match. But clearly they didn't *have* to. It was a free country, with freedom of expression. That's what her parents always told her. Who was to say socks had to match? Certainly not

Melodee Simon. Fara would sooner take advice from a two-ton water buffalo than from Melodee Simon.

"Why do you think people always wear matching socks?" Fara asked her parents that night at dinner.

"That's a good question," her mother said, scooping some spaghetti and meatballs into Fara's bowl. "Why did you always wear matching socks until today?"

"Apart from morning dew?"

"Apart from morning dew."

Fara thought. "It looks nice, I guess, and put together."

"Mm-hmm," her mom agreed. "Matching things do look nice together. Like the curtains and the rug in the living room."

"And like this sauce and these meatballs," her father added, pointing with his fork.

"What does that mean?" asked Mrs. Ross. "Does that mean my homemade tomato sauce—which took two hours to make—is brown and lumpy?"

"No, I'm saying they match because they're both so delicious," Mr. Ross said half convincingly.

Fara thought some more as she slurped a noodle through her lips. She shrugged. "I guess I always matched my socks because that's just what I always did. It's what everyone does. It's what you taught me," she added. "But this is a free country."

"A lot of people do things just because everyone else does them," Fara's mother pointed out. "But that doesn't mean that you can't deviate from the norm."

"What does that mean?"

"Do your own thing," Fara's dad said. "Like Benny," he continued, referring to one of his employees at Lane's Lanes, the bowling alley he owned. "You've seen Benny bowl. He puts the wrong fingers in the ball, and he takes all these extra steps before he throws it. He definitely deviates from the bowling norm." He shook his head in disbelief. "But he always beats me!"

Fara giggled. She liked Benny, and he did look funny when he bowled. But what was even funnier was her dad's expression every time he lost a game to him. "Deviate from the norm," she said. "I like that."

"That's the great thing about personal freedom, Far," her mom continued. "As long as you aren't hurting anybody, you can deviate from the norm as much as you like."

"And what if you are actually *helping* someone when you deviate from the norm? And helping the environment?" Fara asked. She thought of how her socks were something new and different for Jody and the rest of her class. And how they saved just a little bit of water for the wash.

"Well, come on, then, Fara," her dad said with a wink. He took a big bite of sauce and meatball and gave his wife a thumbs-up. "It doesn't get much better than that."

That night before Fara went to bed, she looked at the wall above her bookcase, which was where she taped up post-cards her old babysitter sent her from various countries in Africa, where she was volunteering with the Peace Corps, and letters from her uncle Alan, who had gone to help set up an orphanage in Bosnia. On the top shelf of the bookcase was a pencil case with a picture of Rosa Parks on the cover, which she had bought in the gift shop during a field trip to the Museum of American History, and a report she wrote last year on Franklin D. Roosevelt, plus the round glasses she'd made out of pipe cleaners to wear during her presentation about him for the class. "It seems like a lot of people who make a difference," she wrote in her journal, "start by deviating from the norm."

She tapped her pencil against her lips, and her eyes traveled to the discarded white and gray socks on the top of her laundry basket.

2. Deviating from the Norm

THE NEXT MORNING FARA DECIDED TO MAKE IT clear that choosing socks was a matter of personal freedom. The first sock she chose was a lacy black one that came up to her ankle that she had previously worn only to fancy parties for her mother's law firm. Then she chose the other from her wildest pair of socks, which were striped diagonally, like neon candy canes, three shades of purple and two shades of green. It stretched all the way up to her knee and had separate slots for each of her toes. Since it was warm out and she was once again wearing shorts, all of Harvey Elementary noticed her statement.

Mrs. Ferrara nodded at Fara after telling the class to be original and creative in that morning's writing assignment.

"That's her!" hissed a third grader when passing Fara's class, and all of his friends hesitated by the door, whispering about socks and trying to get a glimpse of Fara's feet.

When the class took a break for snack, Melodee walked by Fara and Jody with her face wrinkled in its usual expression, one of smelling sour milk but not knowing where the odor was coming from. "I think you might not be ready to dress yourself," Melodee said. "Maybe you should ask your mother for help tomorrow."

Fara and Jody couldn't help but laugh at that, seeing as everyone knew how Melodee's mother helped Melodee get anything she wanted. Back in first grade Melodee wanted to quit the Girl Scout troop that Fara's mother ran because Mrs. Ross suggested all of the Scouts donate the clothespin dolls they had made to children in the hospital, and Melodee wanted to keep hers. Ms. Simon saw to it that Melodee brought her clothespin doll home, and she made a show of donating an expensive robotic toy in its place. When Fara's mother told Ms. Simon that the point was to donate something the girls had made, not bought, Ms. Simon said, "Come now, Cheryl. Your little clothespin dolls are precious, but we both know *Melodee's* donation is the greater gift. I think you're the one missing the point. In fact, I think it'd be best if I took over the leadership of this troop myself." When Mrs. Ross did not return as troop leader the next year, it was because Fara had tired of being a Girl Scout, but the Simons were sure they had won the battle.

"I like them," Fara said about her socks. "I chose them myself."

Phillip came by with the snack milk tray. He carefully handed Jody her whole milk and placed Fara's cup of skim on her desk. "Actually, about your socks, Fara . . ." He looked down at Fara's feet as he took a step back and passed a cup of chocolate milk to Melodee at the next table. Hearing the word "socks" again caused Melodee to stick her nose in the air and cross her arms, knocking the cup to the floor and splattering chocolate milk all over her pink sneakers and matching pink socks.

"Oh no," said Phillip. His shoulders dropped. "I guess I should have been looking."

Melodee let out a sigh of disgust before marching away to tell Mrs. Ferrara.

"I'm sorry!" Phillip called after her. He gave Fara and Jody a fretful look and then went up to Mrs. Ferrara's desk without waiting for her to call him. This was the third milk accident since he started carrying the tray last week. Even though everyone liked Phillip too much to say it, they couldn't wait until his term as milk carrier was up. It was almost as bad as when he was put in charge of collecting the jump ropes after gym class—that ended with three students in the nurse's office and Phillip trapped in a tangle of ropes from which it took fifteen minutes and two gym teachers' help for him to escape.

Neither Fara nor Jody was surprised when Phillip came back and reported that his week as milk carrier was ending early.

"Well, what a way to go out!" Jody said.

"Yeah," said Fara. "Of all the people you've spilled milk on, you ended with the best one."

Phillip gave half a smile. "I was just saying that I liked your socks," he said. "It's like that day in second grade when I came in wearing only one sock by accident. Only yours is on purpose." He paused and then looked at Jody and whispered, "Right?"

"Yep," said Jody. "I'm glad Fara did it. We needed something different."

Fara shrugged. "Why do what everybody else does?"

Phillip's smile began to take over the other half of his mouth. "Everybody else carries the tray of milk without dropping it," he said. "I don't want to be like everybody else."

Fara grinned. "Exactly! You're deviating from the norm."

"What does that mean?"

"It means you're doing your own thing. And dropping the milk tray is *definitely* your thing."

Jody patted him on the back. "Nobody else's socks are covered in chocolate milk," she said. "So you helped Melodee deviate from the norm too. We should give you a prize."

3. Taking Sock

FARA STARTING WEARING MISMATCHED SOCKS every day. Some days there were drastic differences between the two (her left would be a white sport sock barely visible above the top of her sneaker, and her right would be one of her mom's old brown knee-highs), and some days there would be hardly any difference at all (her right would be gray with a yellow stripe around the top, and her left would be gray with an orange stripe around the top), since originality and choice were the essence of her statement about freedom.

Whereas most elementary school crazes lasted a week or maybe a month, this one never seemed to lose its appeal. The whole school began to look excitedly to her feet each morning, and students she didn't even know would give her a high five if they especially liked that day's selection. Mike

Dulaney started a contest where people could pay him a quarter to guess what color combination she'd have on the next day, and the winner got half the money (Mike Dulaney kept the rest). Parents began to mill about outside after dropping off their children to see which socks "that original fifth grader" was going to wear. And a bold first grader once stopped Fara on her way home and introduced her to his grandmother. "This is the girl I was telling you about," he said. "She's famous." Fara shook the grandmother's hand and autographed the boy's phonics workbook.

As the end of the school year approached, everybody was still talking about it as if it were new, but for Fara wearing mismatched socks was just part of her routine. In fact, she realized one morning in June, she wasn't really deviating from the norm anymore. She had just made herself a new norm. But it was a norm that everyone she knew would have been sad to see go.

The day before class pictures Mrs. Ferrara reminded the class to dress nicely, but then she faced Fara and added with a wink, "But don't forget to be yourselves." When Fara appeared in a periwinkle sock and a fuchsia sock, Mrs. Ferrara let out a sigh of relief and tousled Fara's neatly combed hair. Fara stood by Jody and Phillip and looped her arms through theirs—the universal sign for wanting to stand next to one another in the picture. "Stand right here in front," Mrs.

Ferrara said to Fara. "Come on, unlink. You'll see Jody and Phillip in a minute. Yes, stand right there between Melodee and Carl." The photographer grinned from behind his camera, but Fara's smile was really only the *ee* of "Cheese," and it was all she could do to keep from holding her nose, since Melodee had put on (too much) perfume for the occasion, and Carl always smelled like cat food. Jody and Phillip spent the rest of the day laughing about how Phillip had tried to give Jody bunny ears in the picture but got his fingers stuck in her hair. It was funny, but Fara didn't see why they needed to recount the story every ten minutes.

"It is so weird," Fara wrote in her journal that night, "how being too original can make you become not original at all. My socks showed that I didn't have to be like everybody else, but now I couldn't be like everybody else even if I wanted to."

The next week Fara couldn't go to school because she had a stomach virus. She called Jody and told her in the morning, but Jody stopped by on her way to school anyway. "I'll get all of your work," Jody said, "and bring it by on my way home."

"Thanks," said Fara. She was happy Jody stopped by, but she wanted to crawl back into bed.

"It's just a twenty-four-hour bug," Jody said matter-of-factly. "It's been going around. I thought about writing about it for the school newspaper, but we already have an article about how the whole first grade got chicken pox a few months ago, and that'd be a lot of negative news."

"True," Fara agreed. "You've got to keep up the school's morale."

Mr. Ross came to the door. "You should get back in bed, Fara. And you should get to school, Jody."

"Well, feel better," Jody said. "I might as well get this day over with. You're out sick, I have a math quiz, and it's Thursday—you know what that means."

"Cello."

"Cello." Jody sighed. She liked playing the cello, she just rarely practiced. "So after school it's homework and then practicing until Boris comes for my lesson." She looked down and saw Fara's bare feet. "And now I'll never know what color socks you were going to wear!"

Fara named the first two colors that came to mind. "Brown and pink."

"Really?" Jody asked. Her face lit up. "Why don't I bring your socks anyway and put them on your chair? For your presence," she said.

Mr. Ross clapped his hands. "That's a great idea."

Fara shrugged. She went upstairs and got a brown sock and a pink sock and gave them to Jody. "Make sure my socks behave," she said.

"I'm sure they'll do all of their work quietly," Jody said,

"but I can't guarantee they'll raise their hand before talking."

When Jody stopped after school to drop off Fara's work and socks, she was bursting with excitement. "Your socks were great!" she said. "Ben won a dollar because he bet on brown and purple, which was close. And Kim invited your socks to her birthday party! Mrs. Ferrara gave them a gold star for being the quietest during silent reading. And Melodee was *so* jealous of the gold star. She kept whining about how she was nice and quiet too. It was really funny."

Fara cocked her head. They were just socks.

"Oh," Jody said. "Phillip got some peanut butter on them during lunch—whoops—so watch where you hold them until you wash them."

Fara laughed. It sounded like a typical day.

All night she kept glancing back at her socks while she completed the work that she'd missed. Did anybody even seem to mind that she was absent? They were happy enough just to have her socks.

Her stomach turned and tightened, even though she had been feeling better since lunchtime.

4. The Originality Award

AS THE YEAR BEGAN WINDING DOWN, THE FIFTH
graders spent more and more time preparing for graduation
and middle school. Phillip joined the Art Committee to
help create banners for the graduation ceremony, though he
was politely asked to unjoin after he knocked over a can of
paint onto two completed banners. Jody worked hard on the
final issue of the school newspaper, and she was selected
to write a speech to read at the graduation ceremony. (Jody
responded to Mrs. Ferrara's invitation with a formal nod of
her head and the statement, "I would be honored," before
grabbing the bathroom pass, running into the hallway, and
screeching.) Jody took her responsibility seriously. During
the class's graduation preparation time each day, she was
either hunched over a draft, her pen scribbling frantically,
or leaning back surveying the class with her "reporter's eye,"

before crossing out a single word and replacing it with something better.

Fara hoped that she would be honored in some way at graduation too, specifically with the Harvey Award for an Outstanding Graduate. At the beginning of the year Mrs. Ferrara had said that the teachers and principal would choose a mature, likable, hardworking, and intelligent young man or woman to receive the Harvey Award at the fifth-grade graduation ceremony. She had pointed out the Harvey Award plaque, which hung outside the main office and had the names of all the past award winners engraved on it. One of the winners, who was now in college, had recently led a successful statewide campaign for requiring all government buildings to use energy-efficient lightbulbs. (Fara had gone door-to-door with her parents to get many people to sign a petition for passing that bill.) The very first winner on the plaque was now the mayor of Stockville; winning the Harvey Award seemed to guarantee making a difference. And Fara thought her name would look nice engraved on a gold plate.

"I really do hope I get the Harvey Award," Fara wrote in her journal while her new dress hung neatly in her closet, ready for graduation the next day. "I worked really hard all year. And I am mature and likable."

The next morning all of the fifth graders paraded onstage in their caps and gowns. All of Jody's work on her speech paid off when she received a standing ovation, even though she had to pause repeatedly when reading it to brush her curls away from her eyes. The first award of the day, the Friendship Award, went to Phillip, and he, too, received a standing ovation for not tripping on his way to receive it. The gym teacher presented an athletic award to Ben Huber, and Mrs. Tully gave Lauryn Washington a medal for winning the district-wide science fair. Then Mrs. Ferrara took to the podium. "I'd now like to honor a very special student who has really made a big impact this year."

Fara took a deep breath and felt her heart start beating quickly. Was Mrs. Ferrara talking about her?

"Fara Ross"—Yes! Yes, she was!—"is a hardworking and intelligent young woman who commits herself to community service and helping others. She is not afraid to stand up for what she believes in." From the front row Jody turned around and beamed at Fara. Both girls crossed their fingers on both hands. Mrs. Ferrara went on. "Toward the end of this year Fara livened up the classroom with her fun footwear." Everyone in the audience chuckled knowingly. A few people applauded, and Fara thought she recognized the claps as belonging to her parents. She looked down at her feet.

"I am therefore proud to present," Mrs. Ferrara said, "a special Originality Award to Miss Fara Ross!"

Everyone cheered and snapped photographs as Fara

walked to the stage in her blue sock and peach sock, which matched her blue mortarboard hat with peach tassel. Her parents cheered loudest of all, and Jody's family were a close second, even though there were many more Gowers than there were Rosses. Fara, grinning, shook Mrs. Ferrara's hand and accepted her award, which was printed on fancy paper that looked like parchment and had a clip-art picture of a pair of socks on it. She loved her mismatched socks. She couldn't believe that because of them the principal created a special award just for her.

But she especially couldn't believe what happened next. The principal went to the microphone and announced that he was going to present the final award, the prestigious Harvey Award for an Outstanding Graduate, to another special young woman who was hardworking and intelligent. Fara felt her shoulders sink at the word "another." *It would be greedy of me to want* two *honors,* she told herself. But who was going to get the Harvey Award? "This fifth grader has dedicated herself to many different causes through-out her time at Harvey Elementary." Who, Fara wondered, besides herself, was dedicated to many different causes? Mike Dulaney once tried to start a petition to make comic books valid choices for book reports, but he was not a she. Jody had written some school newspaper articles sup-porting Fara's causes, such as her movement for the fair treatment of class pets last year, and her unsuccessful campaign to have the school replace the stiff, sandpaper-like brown paper towels in the bathrooms with softer, 100 percent recycled ones (which, Fara admitted, was more for the sake of everyone's hands and noses than the environment). But if it was Jody being honored, surely the principal would be talking about her writing skills, not her dedication to causes. Supporting causes was Fara's domain—it had been ever since that Green Team assembly, which she doubted anyone else even remembered. And even though Melodee and others had sometimes made fun of her for it throughout the years, Fara had resolutely continued to build her reputation as the forward-thinking student who got things accomplished. If someone else in her class was dedicated to causes, Fara wondered why she had yet to meet her; they'd probably get along famously.

Scanning her classmates to pick out another girl dedicated to causes, Fara only partly heard the rest of the principal's introduction, which included something about respect from her peers, diligence in school, and a go-get-'em attitude that summed up what the Harvey Award was all about. She promised herself that whoever this wonderful-sounding person was—Kim Davidson? It sounded like maybe Kim Davidson—she would be happy for her. After all, Fara got the first ever Originality Award, and that was much cooler than having her name engraved on some forty-year-old plaque. But her promise became void the moment the principal announced the winner: "Miss Melodee Simon."

A couple seats away from Fara, Phillip fell out of his chair.

5. Starting Point

MELODEE FLOATED TO THE STAGE AND ACCEPTED her certificate with her face twisted into its sour-smelling version of a smile. Jody spun toward Fara to share a look of utter disbelief, and Phillip, after steadying himself in his seat, did the same.

Fara gulped down her confusion and gave her friends the best shrug she could muster. She curled her toes in her blue and peach socks. She hated her stupid mismatched socks. If it weren't for them, she would be up there shaking the principal's hand.

After the ceremony Melodee and her mother posed by the Harvey Award plaque for a picture that would go in the *Stockville Weekly Reporter* newspaper. Then the photographer asked Fara to place her Originality Award by her feet, and he took a picture of the socks and the award—Fara didn't even have to smile, since the photo wouldn't include anything above her knees.

"Congratulations, Fara," said Linda Simon, Melodee's mother, a large, busty woman with bright red lips and a tight string of pearls around her neck. "How . . . original." She patted Fara on the head.

Fara wanted to do something very immature, like stick out her tongue or push Ms. Simon into the boys' bathroom, but instead she just said, with her own twisted smile, "Thank you. And congratulations to Melodee, too."

Walking home with Jody and Phillip and their families brightened Fara's mood immensely.

"I cannot believe Melodee got that award," Jody said in genuine shock. "I was expecting Kim Davidson maybe, once I realized it probably wasn't you."

"I thought Kim Davidson too!" Fara said. "At least she would deserve it."

Phillip nodded along. "But you got the better one, Fara," he said. "Yours is much more original." He paused. "I mean, it's the Originality Award, but it's also original because it's the Originality Award." He paused again, confused.

"It's much more you," Jody said. "Just like Phillip's award is very Phillip."

"Really?" Phillip asked.

"Of course!" Jody said. "You're a great friend! Everybody likes you."

Phillip blushed.

Fara laughed. "It's true," she said. "And your speech was fantastic, Jode."

Jody beamed. "Thanks."

They walked along in silence for a few seconds, listening to their parents behind them discussing the same things. Then Jody jumped in front of Fara and Phillip. "We're middle schoolers now!" she said.

Back at Fara's house her family raved about her Originality Award all through lunch. Her father took a picture of her uncle Barry holding her upside down by her mismatched feet. Her grandparents gave her a stack of notebooks and pens for middle school, plus twelve pairs of colorful, patterned, or otherwise funky socks. "Supplies for next year," her grandma said with a wink. "You'll make a name for yourself in no time."

Fara thanked them, but she had been hoping for a new bicycle. If her grandparents didn't think she liked socks so much, she might have gotten it.

As they all dug into pieces of a sock-shaped cake, Fara's parents discussed whether Fara would become a philosopher or president. When Fara shrugged and said, "There's no reason I can't be both," her mother gave her a big hug and kiss.

"You're on the right path already," Mrs. Ross said. "Once you're known for doing something good you're in the right place to make a difference."

Uncle Barry nodded. "That's right," he said, chewing a piece of the cake's heel. "It's all who you know."

"What does that have to do with anything?" asked Fara's dad.

Uncle Barry shrugged. "I don't know. It sounded like it fit. Success is ten percent inspiration and ninety percent perspiration. Does that work?"

"Sure," said Mrs. Ross. She turned to Fara and signaled that he was crazy. Fara giggled.

"Are you laughing at me?" Barry asked.

Fara smirked and shook her head.

"I give up," he said. "I'll just keep quiet and eat my sock."

Fara laughed. "I get it," she said. And she did. Now that she was known for her socks, she could use her reputation to do something bigger. Something more noteworthy than receiving the Harvey Award. Something so big—and so far above the ankles—that it could only be achieved by some- one for whom her teacher had had to *invent* an Originality Award. Something that would make a real difference that *she* would be proud of along with everybody else. Now was not the time to stop wearing the mismatched socks, no matter how much they got in her way—now was the time to wear them with pride until that something presented itself.

Satisfied with having a new goal, Fara dug into her roughly sock-shaped slice of sock cake. Now all she had to do was be on the lookout for whatever that goal might be.

6. Something Bigger

FARA DIDN'T HAVE TO BE ON THE LOOKOUT FOR
long. Something bigger came to her a week after graduation
in the form of a twenty-five-year-old man with a ponytail
and a Beatles tie. He was standing on the stage in the auditorium of Stockville Middle School next to a lanky, toupeed
man who Fara could tell was the principal by the way he
stood and eyed the room full of recent fifth-grade gradu-
ates. It was "Welcome, New Middle Schoolers!" morning, a
program for students to find out what was in store for them
come September. Fara and Jody sat together in the middle
of the auditorium. They had walked there together, and
they both were enormously glad that they had, for there
were so many kids there it was impossible to find anybody else they knew among the crowd, including Phillip.
"I hope Phillip found someone to sit with," Jody said.

"Me too," said Fara. "And I hope we can find him after this."

"Who do you think that is?" Jody pointed to the pony-tailed man onstage.

"I was wondering that. I guess he's a teacher?"

"I hope I'm in his class, then."

"Ahem." The principal cleared his throat into the microphone, causing screechy feedback noise that got everyone's attention more efficiently than his clearing his throat. "Welcome, new middle schoolers, to 'Welcome, New Middle Schoolers!' morning."

Someone applauded from the right corner of the room. A few others joined in hesitantly, many students giggled, and Fara and Jody looked at each other; they knew where Phillip was.

"I am the principal of Stockville Middle School, Mr. Cluver. We have a full lineup for you today, to give you a sense of what's in store next year. Usually I begin the day with some opening remarks, but today I am going to let Mr. Zolitski here start, because he has a train to catch. So, here is Mr. Zolitski, one of our social studies teachers, to talk to you about student council. Mr. Zolitski?" He stepped aside to make room for the young man to take the podium. This time more people clapped.

"Good morning," Mr. Zolitski said. "Sorry to change

around the schedule, but I do have a train to catch, and it takes me a while to get to the train station because I ride my bike—much better for the environment than driving a car."

Fara gasped a little. She hoped she was in his class too.

"Anyway, I'm Mr. Zolitski, but you can call me Mr. Z. And I am the adviser for student council. Now, for those of you who don't know what student council is—I don't think they have student council in a lot of your elementary schools—it's a place to make a difference. Student council is for people who have good ideas and want to do something positive for Stockville Middle School."

Fara uncrossed her feet in their violet and polka-dot socks and sat up straighter in her squeaky chair. She had heard of student council, but she had never heard of the people in student council actually doing anything. From the way her older cousin had described it, it sounded like just a big popularity contest. But from Mr. Z.'s description student council at Stockville Middle School seemed like just what she was looking for.

"Now, in some schools student council doesn't really do much. It's just a popularity contest to elect people who then just sit around and feel popular. But not in *my* student council," Mr. Z. said.

Fara's eyes widened. It was like Mr. Z. had telepathy.

"About the second or third week of school I'll be taking

applications for people who want to really do something good for our school. We'll need a president, vice president, secretary, and treasurer for the sixth-grade class. You'll get some more information over the summer, but just to give you a brief idea so you can start thinking about running: The treasurer will be in charge of the money aspect of things. So, math geeks, we need you!" Everyone laughed. "The secretary," Mr. Z. continued, "will take notes at the meetings and be in charge of communicating student council's ideas to the school community. Language arts geeks, that's for you."

Jody sighed. "I'd be secretary," she whispered to Fara, "but I don't think I'll have time for that *and* the school newspaper. Boo."

"The vice president assists the president and does tasks that the president delegates to him or her. And the president, of course, will be the person you all elect to represent your class and make your school a better place for you. All of the class officers should have lots of ideas for things to do for your class and your community, but it's the president who's in charge of accomplishing them."

The blood in Fara's body was rushing around and tingling the tips of her fingers and toes. She couldn't wait for September. Just think how much she could achieve as president! Even just this morning she had noticed that there was no recycling bin in the hall or the auditorium for her empty orange juice box. Recycling would be the first topic in her platform.

"You'll be hearing about a lot of clubs today," Mr. Z. said, "but keep student council in mind. The time commitment depends on how much you want to get done. At a minimum the officers meet with one another and me once a week after school. You may have more meetings for any committees you set up or lead." Fara grinned. She could set up and lead committees! "And then there are more meetings toward the end of the year, when student council plans the sixth-grade dance." Mr. Z. mumbled through that last part and waved his hand in the air to swat away the sixth-grade dance the way he would a mosquito. But some patches of students began to whisper excitedly to each other at its mention. Fara figured that most of the people who decided to run for student council would probably be most interested in planning the dance. She wouldn't mind planning the dance, but if she was too busy instituting important changes, she could just set up a committee to plan the dance and delegate the leadership of it to someone else. She would be such a fair and efficient leader that she would delegate her responsibilities!

"Any questions?" Mr. Z. asked. "Yes, up here in the front."

"What do you have to do to get a position?" asked a voice that sounded like Melodee's with extra sweetener.

"Good question," said Mr. Z. "As I said, in the beginning

of the year you'll have to come get an application from me to run for any position. Then you'll put together a campaign team to help you with the election. You can make posters, stickers, buttons, whatever. Then the whole grade will listen to all of the speeches, and they'll vote for each position. And the winners will be the sixth-grade officers for the year."

Fara nodded and sighed, her thoughts racing. There was nothing Mr. Z. could say that would stop the election from becoming a big popularity contest. That meant she would need more than good ideas to win the election. She would need popularity. She would need socks.

Mr. Z. thanked the students for their time and left to raucous applause. He was certainly the highlight of the morning. The rest of the presenters, who talked about everything from the jazz band to the purpose of guidance counselors, ranged from moderately useful to agonizingly dull. The final speech was from Principal Cluver, though he was hard to hear over the *squeak-squeak-squeak* of seats full of impatient bodies. Even Fara's thoughts had drifted from her potential presidential platform to her potential sandwich fillings for lunch, when the principal said something that brought her attention back to the "New Middle Schoolers" morning. "You are a talented group of students, and we are looking forward to the contributions each of you will make in our community. You have already distinguished yourselves in music, academics, sports, and even, I hear, socks. I cannot wait to see what you all achieve in Stockville Middle School. Thank you for your attention, and we'll see you in September!"

"I can't believe he mentioned you," Jody squealed as everyone got up. "You are so famous. I am so proud to be here with the person who distinguished herself in socks."

"You think it was me he meant?" Fara asked. She felt her face turning red.

"Of course he meant you. Do you see anyone else here with interesting socks?"

Fara looked around as she and Jody made their way out of the auditorium and into the foyer. There were so many people it was hard to see any individual feet, let alone pairs. But that didn't stop the people right around her from pointing at her feet and whispering to one another. *This is good,* she reminded herself. *I need to be known if I want to become president in the fall. Becoming the sock girl now will help me become the class president later.*

"Hey! There's Phillip!" Jody nudged Fara. She jumped. "Phillip! Phillip Ronkel!"

Phillip turned around, bumping right into a girl with brown hair that went down to her waist. "Hey, watch it!" she said.

"Sorry," said Phillip. "Excuse me." He pushed his way through the throngs of students until he reached Fara and

Jody. Two girls followed closely behind him. "Do you think he was talking about you with the socks?" he asked Fara.

"I think so," said Fara with a shrug.

Jody shook her head. "Of course he was! Fara is famous all over."

"Wow," said Phillip.

"Hey, that was you?" one of the girls who had followed Phillip over asked. She looked down at Fara's feet. "Oh yeah. Huh."

"I'm Fara."

"I'm Vicki," the girl said. "Vicki Jordan. And this is Caroline Ma." She pointed to the tiny girl beside her. "Caroline moved here a few months ago from Florida. We both went to Stockville East." Caroline's face was pink. Fara wondered if she was sunburned from having lived in Florida, or if maybe she was one of the people who had distinguished herself in music, academics, or sports.

"Your socks are very nice," Caroline said quietly. "I like them, at least."

"Thanks," said Fara.

Caroline smiled and turned a brighter shade of pink.

"I'm Jody," Jody said. "How do you guys know Phillip?"

"Oh, we were just sitting next to him in there," Vicki said as she pointed to the auditorium. "It's not like we *know* him." She rolled her eyes. "But he said he thought he knew the person the principal mentioned about the socks, so we came to say hi."

Jody grinned. "Well then, hi!" she said. "Wasn't that boring?"

"Ugh," grunted Vicki. "The boringest."

"I liked the part about homeroom," Phillip said.

"What about it?" Fara asked.

"Just about it. What it is. I always wondered what homeroom was."

"Me too," confided Caroline.

Phillip grinned.

The five of them started making their way toward the back door, where Vicki said that she and Caroline were getting picked up. "I can't believe we're going to be walking around this huge place going to different classes. We're like adults," said Jody.

"Finally," agreed Vicki. "I was getting so bored with elementary school."

"I don't know how I'm going to find my way around," said Caroline softly.

"I know," said Fara. "What if you have to go from the first floor on one side of the building to the third floor on the other in four minutes?"

"That's what these are for," Vicki said. She pointed to her running shoes.

"Maybe I'll get those shoes with wheels in them!" said Phillip. "As long as I'm careful not to roll down the stairs."

Jody nudged Fara and pointed to a circle of students Fara didn't recognize. On the outside of the circle, however, was Melodee. "So, do you think you're going to join any clubs?" Melodee was asking a few of the girls in the group.

"Who knows," one girl said.

"Yeah, whatever," said another. They both giggled.

"Oh yeah," said Melodee. "Well, if you want to start a new club or anything, just let me know, because my mom is probably going to be president of the PTA."

The girls Melodee was speaking to seemed to be just as impressed by that as Fara and Jody, who looked at each other and shook their heads. Fara almost felt sorry for her.

Suddenly a boy from the circle pointed and shouted, "Hey, socks!"

The whole group turned and looked at Fara's feet. Fara waved.

"What's your name?" asked the boy.

"Fara Ross."

"So you're the sock person, Fara Ross?"

"Sure," said Fara. Jody patted her on the back.

"Cool. Neil here's the sports person. He's a soccer *star*." He patted one of the other guys—Neil, Fara figured—on the back and pushed him forward. The girls in the circle tittered.

"Oh, come on," said Neil, moving his friend's hand off his back.

"Oh, hey, Fara!" said Melodee, waving as though they were long-lost best friends. "Hi, Jody! Hi, Phil!"

The three of them looked at each other, eyebrows raised. None of them responded.

"Hi, guys," Melodee said again, some anger creeping into her cheeriness.

"Um, hi, Melodee," said Jody finally.

"Have a good summer," said Fara.

"Phil?" said Phillip.

Melodee turned back to the group. "I know them," she said. "They went to Harvey with me. My mom was president of the PTA there, too."

Fara and Jody exchanged knowing glances before moving along down the hallway.

"See you in September!" the boy called after them.

"Yep," shouted Jody.

"Bye, Phil!" Melodee called.

"Who's that?" asked Vicki.

"Oh," said Phillip, "that's Mel."

Fara and Jody laughed all the way home.

7. Summer Socks

SOMETIMES HAVING MISMATCHED FEET OVER the summer was fun. Like when the lifeguards applauded when Fara went to the public pool in mismatched flip-flops. And when she put her green foot on green and her yellow foot on yellow playing Twister at Phillip's birthday party. And when her red-and-white and white-and-blue socks won her a free beach umbrella at a Fourth of July fair. It was also fun spending lazy days lying under the beach umbrella in Jody's backyard reading mysteries, with one magenta foot and one turquoise foot in the air. And kicking the ball all the way to the fence with her smiley-faced foot and touching home plate with her cream-colored foot before the catcher tagged her out.

But sometimes it was trying. Like when she helped organize the shoes and arrange the lighter bowling balls at her dad's bowling alley and had to chat about her socks with everyone who passed. And when she and Phillip found a lost dog, and the owner was so taken by Fara's socks that she forgot even to thank them for returning her pet. And when the ice cream man gave her a strawberry and vanilla twist cone to match her socks instead of the plain vanilla one she had asked for, and she had to throw it away after eating as much of the vanilla part as she could, since even the *thought* of strawberries made Fara want to puke ever since she'd bit into a moldy strawberry last summer.

Why, *why*, Fara wondered angrily all those times, did people think that because her socks didn't match socks were all she cared about? Her own family members were interested only in her socks at her grandparents' anniversary party. Even her twelve-year-old cousin whom she hadn't seen in two years and had been looking forward to seeing at the party for weeks, wanted to talk not about school and books and movies, but about Fara's socks.

"And then it got even worse," Fara said in an eerie voice. It was a rainy first day of August, and she and Jody and Phillip were lounging around in Fara's living room. They were playing Jody's favorite game, which involved going around in a circle to make up a story, one sentence at a time. This round's story was a scary one, and thanks to Fara's sentence, the three main characters—Felicia, Jenny, and Pharaoh (they always had trouble coming up with a boy's name close to Phillip's)—were about to find themselves in an even worse situation.

"They saw that one of the doors in the dark hallway was open a little bit, and there was noise coming from inside," Phillip said.

Jody continued, "So Jenny, Felicia, and Pharaoh walked toward the door and pushed it open to find their worst nightmare: that they were guests at a birthday party—"

"A birthday party?" said Fara and Phillip together.

"How is that someone's worst nightmare?" Fara added.

"Let me finish," Jody said. "They were guests at a birthday party . . . for Melodee Simon!"

"Nooo!" cried Phillip dramatically.

"Make it end!" Fara wailed.

Jody let out a sinister cackle.

"They had to stay for the whole party," Fara said, "and give Melodee presents!"

"And when the party finally ended," Phillip said, "four *hours* later, they knew that if they could live through that, they could survive anything."

"So they ran straight out of the scary mansion, past the crying ghosts and the old man with the bloodsucking machine, and the robots with chainsaws that were guarding the exit, all the way to safety. The end."

They all laughed and applauded. The ending was a little bit quick, but this was their best story yet.

"Speaking of birthday parties," said Jody, "what are you going to do for yours, Far?"

Fara rubbed her hands together. She had been think-ing about what she wanted to do for her birthday for a long time, and the night before she had finally circled her deci-sion from the list in her journal. "Well," she said, "my cousin once told me about a birthday party that she had at a pizza place. Everybody gets to go behind the counter and make their own pizza—roll the dough and add whatever toppings and everything—and stick it in the oven. And then eat it. I think it sounds really fun."

"And yummy," said Phillip.

"Pizza is good," Jody said slowly, "but you know what's even better?" She made a drumroll noise on her lap. "Socks!"

"Yeah!" said Phillip. "Pizza has nothing to do with socks."

"So?" said Fara. *Exactly,* she thought.

"So, you *have* to have a sock party. A mismatched-socks party. You could give out socks as favors. And we could play sock games." Clearly Jody had been thinking about Fara's birthday party a lot too.

Mrs. Ross stuck her head out of the kitchen, where she'd

been doing some work at the table. "Like pin the socks on the feet," she suggested.

"Yeah, and a team game where you have to throw balled-up socks into a moving laundry basket."

"A laundry-themed birthday party?" Fara said dully.

"Not laundry, socks," Phillip explained patiently.

"I think that's a fabulous idea!" Mrs. Ross said. "A real lot of fun. Dad's going to love it."

"I still kind of want the pizza party, though," Fara said.

"We can have pizza here. I can even buy dough and you can all make it. You could make your slices in the shape of socks. Ha!"

Fara sighed loudly, but everyone else was so busy discussing the details of the sock party that they didn't hear her. *The party will probably be fun,* Fara thought, *but I just wish it didn't have to be about socks, like everything else.* But for everyone else's sake—and her own, if she was serious about running for president in a few weeks—she decided to focus on the first part of her thought.

"How does that sound, honey?" asked her mother.

Fara hadn't been listening, but three excited faces were turned toward her, awaiting a response.

"It'll be great!" said Phillip.

"Yeah," Fara conceded, making her mouth into a smile. "It'll be great."

*   *   *

The sock party was a huge success. Ten guests showed up—a record number for Fara's birthday, since August 18 was a prime time for summer camp or family vacations—including Vicki and Caroline, the girls they had met at middle school orientation. Everyone came in socks and no shoes, but so as not to step on her toes, only Fara's were mismatched. They played pin the socks on the feet, and they made personal sock-shaped pizzas, as promised. Phillip and his father brought a piñata. Fara hugged Phillip and said, "Thank you!" when she saw it because it was shaped like a donkey and not a sock. But when Mike Dulaney managed to break it open, lots of balled-up socks came falling out instead of candy. Even though she was sock sick, Fara had to admit that that was pretty clever.

In the backyard her parents laid out a big banner that said HAPPY 11ᵀᴴ BIRTHDAY, FARA! and everyone took off their socks, stepped in trays of different-colored paint, and put their footprints on the banner. (Phillip forgot to step in the tray of soapy water afterward, so he also left his footprints on the grass all the way back to the house door, where Mrs. Ross caught him and turned him around to wash off.) While they were stepping on the banner, Fara's uncle hid everybody's discarded socks around the house, and they had to search for them after lunch. Since more than half of the socks were white, most people ended up with socks that didn't fit. When Jody squeezed Fara's hand and cried, "This is the best birthday party ever! And all thanks to socks!" Fara had to grin, squeeze back, and agree.

But then, as the party was winding down and parents were beginning to arrive, Fara started opening her gifts.

The first was from Kim Davidson: eleven pairs of funky-colored socks. "Oh, thanks," said Fara, fairly earnestly. Kim smiled and shrugged.

The next one she opened was from Caroline: a pair of earrings that looked like little socks. "Oh, cute. Thanks, Caroline."

Caroline turned red and said, "You're welcome, Fara."

Then she opened Phillip's gift. A Red Sox shirt. "Get it?" he said.

She opened a long, skinny box from Uncle Barry. It was a tie with pictures of socks on it. Fara looked up at him and raised her eyebrows. He shrugged. "I know you're a girl, and girls don't wear ties," he said, "but I saw it and couldn't resist." Fara thanked him, but she was getting worse at pretending socks were the gift of choice for every eleven-year-old. She even felt guilty thinking she had to give one of these presents to Goodwill; it seemed unfair that some other kid would wind up with stupid sock stuff.

The rest of the gifts were devastatingly similar. A

mismatched pair of stockings filled with candy, thirty-three pairs of socks, a miniature chest of drawers for socks, a clock in the shape of a sock, a sock-shaped lamp, another set of the same sock earrings, and a poster of a dog wearing socks.

That settled it. Fara officially hated socks.

If she hadn't received a package from Stockville Middle School the next day with information about after-school activities, including student council, she might have ended her socky statement right then. "These socks had better pay off," she wrote in her journal that night while eating the candy that she considered to be her only good birthday present. "And then once I win, I'll just have to do so many good things for the school and the community that people will have so much to talk about they'll forget to even mention socks." Or maybe, she thought hopefully, her new classmates would notice her feet enough to recognize her when voting for student council, but not enough that they'd *really* care. Sure, they'd enjoyed her birthday party, but mature sixth graders couldn't be *that* interested in socks, right?

8. Freedom of Footwear

WRONG. BY THE THIRD DAY OF SCHOOL EVERY-
one had something to say about Fara's feet.

"Hey! Socks!" said Dennis Richardson in homeroom.

Tania Farucci stared and then whispered to Diana Klein during first period.

Vicki nodded and said, "You're still doing it!" during second period.

Soccer-player-Neil smiled a little; then he pretended he was looking at a stain on the floor when his friend saw him smiling during third period.

"Soccer-player-Neil smiled at you a little, but then he pretended he was looking at a stain on the floor when his friend saw him smiling!" Jody gushed during lunch.

Mrs. Henderson saluted her at the start of fifth period.

Melodee pointed out the way *her* outfit matched *perfectly* during sixth period.

The gym teacher chuckled and said, "You're something else, Ross," during seventh period.

Zoë Wilson pretended to bow down to her feet during eighth period.

By the second week of middle school even the best mornings took a turn for the worse when she opened her sock drawers. Even if a wonderful song was playing when her clock radio went off and it became the soundtrack for her wonderful dream until she slowly, easily drifted into consciousness and realized that her favorite T-shirt was freshly washed and it was macaroni day at lunch and she knew her science teacher was going to be absent—even those days turned slightly soggy when it came time to choose socks.

While everyone else in sixth grade was slowly, gradually shaping their middle school reputations, Fara felt like hers was already sprayed in permanent paint on the side of the building, written in permanent marker inside every bathroom stall, and printed in permanent ink next to her name on every attendance list: Fara Ross, Sock Girl. So while Fara was thinking about the things most of the sixth graders did, like homework and television and who held hands in the hallway, she was also thinking about society and individuality and freedom.

"No one really knows where their classrooms are, and we barely know each other's names," Fara wrote in her journal. "But everyone knows about my socks! I want freedom of choice, freedom of expression, freedom of footwear! I bet I'm the only person in the whole world whose life is based so much around something like socks."

She could think of a million things more important to Stockville Middle School than socks. Well, maybe not a million, but a lot. Things like starting a recycling program, since there weren't even blue bins for paper, not to mention that cardboard lunch trays, plastic bottles, and unwanted pieces of fruit all got dumped into the same trash cans. And things like making sure there weren't bugs crawling on the beef stew on the lunch line. And things like trying again for softer, environmentally friendly paper towels in the bathrooms. Fara's campaign platform kept growing along with her socky popularity. So did her confidence in her ability not only to win the election, but to make a bigger difference for the better once she was elected.

"I want to make a difference," Fara told Mr. Z. when she handed in her presidential application after school.

"Then you're just the woman for the job," he said. "You'll just have to beat out the other woman for the job. . . ." He took out a folder labeled STUDENT COUNCIL APPLICATIONS—

PRESIDENT and looked at the name on the top of the only other application. "Melodee Simon."

Fara wiggled her toes in her beige sock and her paisley sock. She smiled. The match wouldn't even be close.

9. Young Journalist

JODY WAS OFF THE WALL WITH EXCITEMENT.
She bounded out of Mr. Francis's room, rounded the corner, and, in an overzealous hug attempt, crashed into Fara, propelling them both into a panel of lockers. "Guess what!" she said, panting and tucking her brown curls behind her ears. "Guess *what!*"

Fara rubbed her elbow. "What?"

"Oh my God, did you hurt your elbow?" Jody asked. "I'm so sorry! I didn't mean to hurt you, but I was just so excited!"

"I can tell," Fara said. "About what?"

"Well, Mrs. Ferrara—our old teacher, Mrs. Ferrara!—she nominated me for this Young Journalist competition. She didn't tell me she nominated me because she didn't want me to be upset if I didn't win, and she figured that I could always just not accept it if I did win and I didn't want to do it, so she just nominated me without telling me—and I won!"

"Awesome!" said Fara. "What do you win?"

Jody brushed her curls away from her face again and cleared her throat. "I am now the official Young Journalist for the *Stockville Weekly Reporter*."

"What?" shouted Fara.

"Yep!" shouted Jody. "I get to write articles, and they'll print them with my name on them and everything!"

"Shut up!" shouted Fara.

"Nope!" shouted Jody. Her red sweatshirt came untied from around her waist and slipped to the ground. As she picked it up she said, "And I get to talk to real journalists, and they'll teach me things about writing and help me with my articles."

"That is so cool!" Fara yelled.

"I know!" Jody shrieked.

Mrs. Henderson stepped into the hallway. "Congratulations, Miss Gower," she said. "But could you and Miss Ross please keep your excitement to a respectful decibel level? Students are trying to take a makeup test in here."

"Sorry!" shouted Jody, retying the sweatshirt quickly and sloppily.

Fara took her best friend's arm and pulled her toward the stairwell. "Come on, Young Journalist. There won't be people taking makeup tests outside."

"Geez, I hope not." Jody raced ahead and held the door

for Fara. It had been unusually cold for September for a few days now, and as Fara stuffed her hands inside the sleeves of her sweater she hoped that this was only a weird spell and that Stockville would see some more of summer before next June. Between her jeans and her sneakers one of her ankles was nice and warm inside a fuzzy pink sock, but the other was feeling the wind beneath a thin sock that was navy blue with teal stripes.

If Jody noticed that it was cold out, she didn't show it, and her red zippered sweatshirt stayed tied around her waist while she bounced alongside Fara. "I can't believe Mrs. Ferrara never told me that she nominated me," she said. "She had to submit stuff last *year*. And then she told Mr. Francis today that I won. But I guess it was pretty smart, because I would have been so bummed if I hadn't won. And now this is just a huge, amazing, fantastic surprise! I mean, this is so *big*."

Fara grinned. "I bet they'll love you and tell you to skip school and just start working for them," she said.

"Yeah, right," said Jody. "But that would be so cool!"

"Don't become so famous that you have to move to the city and leave me here."

"Oh, of course not," said Jody. "At least not until your student council campaign is over. And I guess it'd only be smart to graduate from middle school. I mean, I might as well."

"Right. And when I win the election, I'll need you around to write really good articles about all the stuff I put into place."

"And when you become president of the United States, I'll write really good articles about the stuff you do for the country." She stopped at the corner and placed her hand over her heart. "And I will never muckrake you."

"Thanks," Fara said with a salute. She glanced down her block and shivered. "Well, congratulations. Don't be so excited that you forget to come to the brainstorming session tonight."

"I won't . . . ," she promised. "Well, maybe you'd better call and remind me."

Fara nodded. After one more bouncy hug and many hyper waves good-bye, she managed to break away from Jody to head home. But even from around the corner and down the street she heard a faint "Woohoo!"

10. Some Socky Slogans

FARA MADE SOME ORANGE KOOL-AID AND put out some cups. She wasn't very excited for this meeting because she wasn't a big fan of group work. But at least she had gotten to choose her group. She couldn't really go wrong with Jody on her team, or with Phillip, as long as there was nothing breakable involved. And she was glad to have their new friends Vicki and Caroline on board. They both seemed so nice, though Vicki did most of the talking for the two of them.

Fara heard a car door slam and went to the door to find both Vicki and Caroline. "Hey, guys. Come on in. But take off your shoes, please."

"Hey, Fara," Vicki said as she entered. "I brought Sour Straws, and Caroline brought carrots. And she wore something special for tonight's meeting."

Caroline stepped into the house, her face growing redder by the second. Up until recently Fara had thought that Caroline might be permanently sunburned. But one afternoon Fara spotted her doing English homework quietly in a corner of the library and realized that Caroline's face wasn't always red; it was only when she was around people. In the one class Fara had with her, math, Caroline never, ever raised her hand, but if Mrs. Velasquez called on her, she always whispered the right answer. And Fara noticed that she always finished her work first. Vicki went around saying that Caroline had rosacea (whatever that meant), but Fara and Jody liked to joke that Caroline should be their school's mascot, since her flushed face and black hair made for a perfect Stockville Red Fox.

"Thank you for having us," Caroline said to the carpet as she removed her shoes and placed them neatly against the wall.

"No problem." Fara caught sight of her small feet: one in a yellow sock and one in a sock that was slightly off-yellow, probably from her mother having accidentally washed it with the whites.

"I think she's got the right idea," Vicki said. "I think we should all wear socks like you for the entire campaign."

Fara laughed. *Stupid socks,* she said to herself. "You guys can go sit in the kitchen," she said to her guests. "Oh, here's Phillip."

He walked up carrying a folder full of papers and a box of crackers with cheese. On his way up the stairs his heel came out of his loafer, causing his foot to slip a little. With an "Oh no" he threw his arms out to block his fall, crushing the box of crackers and causing the folder to fly open and the papers to settle around him. Fara smiled at him from the doorway.

"I really walked the whole way here without tripping once," Phillip said. "Honest."

Fara shook her head and stepped outside to help him pick up the papers. One of them had a sketch of a stick figure wearing mismatched socks. She held it up to him and raised her left eyebrow.

"I was doing some plans for posters," he said, pulling it away and stuffing it back into the folder. "Just trying to get a head start."

"Cool," Fara said.

Jody jumped out of her family's minivan just as Phillip moved inside. She had a pencil tucked behind her ear and a spiral memo pad in her hand.

"You look like such a professional!"

Jody grinned. "Well, I *am* managing a campaign here. And I'm a reporter now too. You should have seen me before," she said while she removed her shoes. "I put the pencil in my hair because I thought that looked *really* professional, but then I forgot about it and took out my ponytail, and the pencil got lost in my hair for, like, five minutes. Oh, and I brought Cheez Doodles. And do you think I could maybe borrow a pen? I don't really like writing in pencil."

Fara laughed and nodded. She started to go to the kitchen, but Jody touched her shoulder.

"Can we hang out for a little after the meeting?"

Fara shrugged. "Sure."

"Great! I have an idea that I want to get started on right away."

"What is it?"

Jody raised her eyebrows twice. "Just wait," she promised. "We'll talk about it after the meeting."

The team assembled around the kitchen table and munched on carrots, Cheez Doodles, cheese and crackers, Sour Straws, and orange Kool-Aid.

Fara's father arrived home from work at the bowling alley and stopped in the kitchen, asking, "Can't you kids eat anything that isn't orange?"

"We've got Sour Straws," offered Vicki. "They're all sorts of colors—radioactive red, bodaciously bitter blue. . . ."

Mr. Ross shook his balding head, kissed Fara's forehead, and poured himself a glass of Kool-Aid.

"How's Lane's Lanes, Mr. Ross?" asked Jody, who found

Fara's parents' occupations much more interesting than her parents', which were a psychologist and a full-time mom. She especially liked to talk about Lane's Lanes, which Fara's dad had taken over when his dad retired. It was called Lane's Lanes because when Fara's grandpa opened it, it was on a street called Lane Road. But when the area around the alley got built up around the time Fara was born, the street name changed to New Town Road. Mr. Ross kept the name the same, even though it didn't make much sense anymore.

"Oh, it's the usual," he replied between sips of his Kool-Aid. "Actually, a league for young moms started this afternoon, and a lot of them really appreciated the new soy muffins at the snack counter! They wanted more flavors, and they suggested some exotic ones, like cornflower cranberry." Before going on to list more muffin flavors, however, he noticed Fara's *Please go upstairs and talk about work later* look and said, "But I don't want to keep the campaign team from their duties." He winked at Fara and took his drink, the newspaper, and the mail up to his bedroom.

Jody said she would write everything down, so Phillip offered to be the timekeeper.

"Okay, Mrs. Henderson," said Vicki, referring to their social studies teacher, who, when assigning group work, always gave each group member a specific role with a cheesy title, like Ready Reporter, Time Tracker, and Presentation Pro. "This isn't school," said Vicki. "We don't need to divide up into dumb jobs."

Phillip turned as red as Caroline. "I know," he said quietly. "That's why I was joking."

Fara knew that an ideal student council president would have to make everyone feel important. She practiced by telling Phillip that they could, actually, use a timekeeper. "That way you can keep us all on track and make sure this doesn't take too long. But I think you're right, Vicki; we don't really need a Materials Maven."

Caroline smiled at her. "But we'll all be Keen Contributors," she joked quietly.

"That's why you would be the perfect leader," Jody said. She scribbled down notes in her memo pad. "You are so friendly and you solve problems. Now if only that was a catchy slogan." She tapped her pen against her lips. "Fara Is Friendly." She made a face similar to the one she'd made after sucking on a Sour Straw. "That's so boring." She tried again: "Fara Is a Friendly Problem Solver."

Fara shook her head. She thought that sounded like something out of a third-grade math workbook: *Help Fara the Friendly Problem Solver solve the following word problems*. "It can be something simple," she said. "And direct."

"No," said Vicki. "Everybody knows you because you're original. So it can't just be, like, Fara Ross for President."

"Fara Ross Will Be an Original, Friendly, Problem-Solving President!" announced Jody.

They all shook their heads, even Caroline.

Vicki banged her hands on the table. "Fara Ross Is Our Boss." She sat back in her chair and crossed her arms to show their work was done.

"Gross," said Jody, who had accidentally chewed on the wrong side of her pen.

Vicki rolled her eyes. "Well, it's better than what you came up with."

Fara licked all of the cheese off a Cheez Doodle. "I don't really want to be a boss, though," she said. "I want to be a leader."

"Whatever," said Vicki, rolling her eyes so far back they looked like they might disappear. "I said it because it rhymes. Fara Ross Is Our Leader doesn't rhyme."

"And it sounds like something someone would say when they knock on your door and give you pamphlets," Jody said. "You know, those guys who carry briefcases and wear those nice clothes? What are they called?"

"Suits?" suggested Phillip.

Fara laid her cheek on her hand. "Well, why don't I tell you guys my ideas and then we can go from there?"

Caroline sat upright and said, "Good idea."

"Why?" said Vicki. "We're thinking of slogans."

Before Fara could protest, Jody suggested Fara Is Fair-a, and everybody agreed that they were getting nowhere.

Phillip announced that it was eight fifteen.

Vicki said, "It might as well be Wear Mascara and Vote for Fara."

Fara laughed. "Or, Like to Floss? Vote for Ross."

Jody loved them both. "You'll get all the votes from people who want to be dentists," she reasoned.

"Oh yeah," said Vicki, looking at her like she had said Fara would get all the votes from people who wore underwear on their heads. "Because there are *loads* of those."

Fara shook her hands in the air. "I think we're taking the wrong approach here," she said.

"I agree," said Caroline. "What do you want to do if you win?"

Fara reached for the spiral notebook in which she'd formulated her platform. On the cover her mom had drawn the letters of her name out of socks. It wasn't a particularly good drawing—Mrs. Ross often joked (with, Fara thought, some seriousness) about having become a lawyer to sue the fifteen art schools that had denied her admission—but it was clear enough that the items were supposed to be socks and that they were supposed to spell "Fara."

Vicki banged on the table. "Yes! We're overlooking the number one thing we should be thinking about. Socks!"

Phillip excitedly took out his sketches. "We should have a picture of Fara like this," he said, pointing to the stick figure, "and then the slogan on top."

"Or she could be saying the slogan in a speech bubble," said Vicki, "like in a cartoon."

"Or there could be a caption," offered Jody, "like in a newspaper."

"But what will it say?" asked Caroline.

The table became silent except for the sound of Phillip chewing on a carrot (which he put down after he realized that the table was silent except for the sound of him chewing on a carrot). Fara read through the outline of her platform in her head, trying to think of something catchy that dealt with the issues. But the best she could come up with was F.A.R.A.— For A Recycling Association, and she didn't need the others' input to know it wasn't exactly what they were looking for.

Then Jody let out a single laugh. Then she said, "Sorry," closed her mouth, and took a loud breath through her nose. But on the exhale she started giggling, and this time she couldn't regain her composure. Everyone looked at her expectantly. "Vote for Fara and School Won't Sock!" she managed to huff through her laughter. Then she burst out laughing even harder and ran to the bathroom.

The whole campaign team roared, partly over the slogan, but mostly over the fact that Jody had had to run to the bathroom. Vicki banged on the table with each loud "HA!" and Phillip dropped his poster design and slipped on the kitchen tile trying to run after it, which only made everybody laugh harder. Caroline's face was the reddest Fara had ever seen it, and her shoulders shook uncontrollably even though she wasn't making any noise through her smile. Fara laughed until her stomach hurt, and Jody's sheepish return didn't help her catch her breath.

When they finally settled down, Vicki announced that that slogan was brilliant. "It works for everything," she explained. "If you want to talk about cafeteria food, you just say Vote for Fara and the Food Won't Sock."

Fara brightened at the thought of actually incorporating her ideas into the posters. And the slogan was definitely catchy.

Phillip started to draw a lopsided speech bubble outside the stick figure's mouth. He stopped halfway through and said, "But wait. If everyone votes for Fara, then school *will* sock. Because she's famous for socks."

Jody shook her head as she wrote it all down. "It doesn't matter, Phillip," she said. "It's just a slogan. No one will think about it that carefully."

Vicki made "Mmm" sounds through her Kool-Aid, which

they finally understood after she swallowed. "Bid Fara-well to Socky Class Presidents!"

Everybody laughed, including Phillip, until he said, "But wait. Fara *will* be a socky president."

Fara crossed her arms. "Why are you on my campaign team if you think I'd make a socky president, huh?"

"No," explained Phillip seriously. "I mean that *you* are socky."

Caroline gasped.

"Because you sock."

They all laughed.

"No, I mean we can't say that you won't sock, because everybody knows that you already do!"

Vicki sprayed orange Kool-Aid all over the table, which sent Jody running to the bathroom again.

After calming down and getting paper towels, Fara patted Phillip on the back and told him they got it. When Jody returned, they got serious (as serious as they could when discussing the various ways in which Fara wouldn't "sock") and listed a handful of slogans for the first round of posters, which were due to Mr. Z. by the following Thursday. Jody said she'd type up the minutes from the meeting ("See, I knew we could use a timekeeper!" said Phillip) and bring four printouts to school tomorrow, just in case people forgot the slogans or their assignments. They wrapped up just as they heard the distinct toot of the Mas' Volvo in the driveway.

Caroline sat on the carpet and buckled her Hush Puppies, while Vicki stuffed her feet into her permanently laced Nikes. Fara's parents waved to Mrs. Ma from the doorway and, just to make Fara wish she'd held the meeting somewhere else, bid the team "Fara-well" (they'd heard from upstairs). Caroline offered Phillip a ride home, and Vicki suggested, on a final note, that they all wear mismatched socks for the length of the election period, starting tomorrow.

While Jody argued that they shouldn't because it had to remain unique to Fara, and her parents joined the debate on opposing sides, Fara wondered, with mounting frustration, how her friends would feel after wearing mismatched socks for three weeks. Would Phillip become even clumsier, embarrassed with all of the attention, and would Vicki start to complain about the pressure to think creatively? Maybe the fact that her sock collection would give her headaches would cause Caroline to quietly grow angrier and angrier until she exploded with a delicate, red pop. If they understood, Fara thought, then maybe it would be easier to stop. Or at least it'd be nice to have a support group. She chuckled at the thought of Sock Support.

"Thank you for having us," said Caroline to Fara's parents.

"Oh," said Vicki, "yeah, thanks."

"Bye," said Phillip to Fara. "I'll start drawing right away."

"Yeah," said Vicki as she pushed him out the door, "and your drawings had better not sock."

11. The Eruption of Mount Saint Fara

AFTER THE TEAM HAD GONE, JODY CALLED home and was told that she was going to get picked up at nine thirty, so she said they had better get to work on the next project, which she still hadn't revealed. She grabbed the remaining Sour Straws and led the way up to Fara's room.

"So I read the entire information packet about my Young Journalistship," Jody said as she settled on Fara's bed. "I get to write one article a month for the whole school year. And I can spend two days a month in the *Weekly Reporter* office getting an insider's view of how a real newspaper operates."

"Very cool."

"I know. In the beginning I'll probably just watch. But after a few times they might ask me to help them with stuff, like laying out the articles and things!"

"This job was made for you."

Jody blushed. "Thanks. So I want my first article to come out really soon. Like, next week. And I thought of a really good thing to write it about."

"Oh yeah? It's too bad Mr. Fanticelli hasn't gotten the volcano to work yet," Fara said, referring to their science teacher, who had spent the past period and a half pouring fake lava into a plaster volcano and trying, unsuccessfully, to make it spray back out. "Then you could write about that."

"That *would* be news," said Jody. "But I love Mount Saint Failure. I hope he keeps trying for at least another day or two."

"Me too. He didn't even realize he forgot to give us homework today!"

"I know!" said Jody. "But anyway. My article. I've got to pick a topic that interests kids our age. You know, like preteen issues or middle school life or something. But they suggest starting small with something you know a lot about so that you can write accurately. According to Gary . . . Hodas? Hoagie? Ho-something—that's the key to good writing."

"Who's Gary Ho-something?"

"He's the main editor at the *Stockville Weekly Reporter*. There was a whole page by him in the pamphlet I got."

"So, what are you going to write about?"

Jody grinned. She made a drumroll noise. "I'm going to write about you!"

Fara didn't understand. "Me?"

"Uh-huh! I have to write about something I know, and what do I possibly know better than you? Well, maybe how to write articles, but that would be a dumb topic for my first article, don't you think? It would make me seem really stuck up. That's probably what Melodee would do, even though she doesn't really know how to write articles. But you know what I mean. Anyway, you're perfect to write about! And the research will be fun because it will just be talking to you."

"Wow. I guess you've got this all planned out, then?"

"Yep. And I figured we could start the interview right now." She flipped open her memo pad and crossed her legs. "If that's okay with you, of course."

"I guess so," Fara said, catching some of Jody's excitement. Even though no one was taking her picture, she suddenly felt the need to comb through her hair with her fingers. It would be kind of cool to have a whole article about her in the town newspaper. She could talk about her plans for the recycling program and how they could lower pollution if everybody in Stockville got involved. "As long as you're sure you can't find something more interesting to write about than me," she added. "I mean, this isn't for just the school paper."

"Come on, Fars. You're the most interesting person I know."

Fara grinned.

Jody continued, "You and your socks."

Fara felt everything drop—her hands from her hair, the corners of her mouth, her shoulders, her stomach. "You're going to write about my socks?"

"Of course, what did you think?" Jody bounced on the bed. She poised her pen on the paper. "Okay, Miss Ross. Question number one: What made you start wearing mismatched socks? Was it an accident?"

"You know the answer to that, Jody," she said, suddenly wishing her friend would go home and she could just go to sleep.

"Not on the record I don't. This is going on the record, by the way."

"Well, for the record, then." Fara sighed. "At first it was kind of an accident. But then everyone noticed it, and it got me thinking about individuality and freedom. So I kept wearing them because I wanted to make a statement," she said without inflection. "And a difference. I thought that I could express my individuality and freedom by wearing mismatched socks."

If Jody noticed Fara's unenthusiastic tone she didn't show it; rather she was scribbling so fast that Fara was waiting for the paper to catch on fire. She looked up at Fara and said, grinning, "Off the record, that's why you're so cool, you know," and then went back to writing. When she'd finished, she asked, "Do you feel you accomplished that goal?"

Fara thought again, this time a little bit more sincerely. "I guess I did for other people," she said, "but it's funny. Because it kind of became the opposite."

"The opposite how?" Jody asked in her best interviewer voice.

There was something about the way Jody asked— as though it were all so simple—that made something burst inside Fara. This whole conversation was too much. Her shoulders flew up again. "How?" she said loudly. "I became so known for it that I can't do anything else! It's what everybody thinks about me all the time!" And then it all came tumbling out. How she'd gotten sick of socks but couldn't do anything about it. How she was sick of sock-related conversations and sock-related jokes. How she hated having people stare at her feet all day, and how she especially hated how Mrs. Velasquez had developed a bonus math problem to figure out what fraction of Fara's socks had patterns on them. Her passion mounting, the words just kept coming, spilling out and spraying all over like the contents of a giant water balloon that slips through your fingers before you can tie it. And whenever she ran out of air, she just took a deep breath and let the words start splattering again, until she'd voiced to her best friend what her journal and mind had been burdened with for months. Right up to that very night with those very slogans and the very topic for that very article that that very friend wanted to write.

And when she finally finished, breathless and sore from throwing her arms about, she took notice of Jody, whose eyes were wide and lips were slightly open, her pen suspended halfway through the word "opposite."

"I'm sorry," said Fara.

"I'm sorry," said Jody. "I had no idea."

"I'm sorry," said Fara. "But you were just so into it. I didn't want you to be disappointed."

"But you've been so angry!"

"It's really not that bad," said Fara. Neither of them spoke for a few seconds, then they both started laughing at the absurdity of that statement.

"So just stop," said Jody. "I'll support you. Socks shmocks!"

Fara shook her head. "Weren't you listening?" she said, giggling. "The election."

Jody tapped her pen on her lips. "I'll help you figure something out." She looked at her notes before flipping the pad closed. "But in the meantime, maybe you can start a registry for Hanukkah. Like how my aunt registered for her wedding so everyone would buy her the presents she wanted. You can register somewhere that doesn't sell anything socky. Like . . . the zoo."

"The zoo?"

"I don't know."

Fara laughed. "What could people buy me at the zoo?"

"I don't know! A mug in the shape of a giraffe? At least nothing that has to do with socks."

"They'd probably find some socks with cartoon zebras on them."

"But they couldn't buy them if they're not on the list of stuff you register for. Sheesh."

Fara's sock clock showed that it was just past nine thirty. Jody got up and gave Fara a tight hug.

"Thanks," Fara said.

"Yep. We'll figure it out. I've already got an idea in the works."

Fara nodded and tried to smile. *Uh-oh,* she thought.

"And next time you hate something, tell me before you . . . blow up. Or what do volcanoes do? Erupt!"

"I did sort of erupt, didn't I?"

"Mr. Fanticelli would have been so happy."

"Mount Saint Fara," Fara said with a laugh.

After seeing Jody out and kissing her parents good night, Fara got ready for bed. *Boy, it felt good to erupt,* she thought while brushing her teeth. She should have done that months ago. Knowing that she had to be creative with her footwear tomorrow didn't even bother her, since Jody was finally on her side. She clicked off her sock-shaped lamp and dreamed of the eruption of a giant sock-filled volcano, a vibrant cotton storm that dropped her socks far, far away.

12. Publicity

WHEN FREEDOM ISN'T FREEDOM

A Preteen Spotlight

by Young Journalist Jody Gower

Every morning at Stockville Middle School, the halls buzz with excitement over Fara Ross's feet. Not because they smell bad or because they are radiantly beautiful, but because each one is wearing something different and interesting. Fara is a normal sixth grader, but there is nothing normal about her socks. By wearing ones that don't match every day for months, Fara Ross has made a positive name for herself among Stockville's young adults, and she has inspired others with her originality.

"I wanted to make a statement and a difference," said Fara of her noble intentions in a recent interview. "I thought that I could express my individuality and freedom by wearing mismatched socks." She started doing it in April, when she was still in fifth grade at Harvey Elementary School, and she hasn't worn a matching pair or the same combination a single day since then.

And she certainly has created a buzz. Most of the students love it, some of them hate it, but everybody knows about it.

"I saw them once! Right up close!" bragged a fourth grader at Harvey. "She was at her locker and I dropped a book so I could bend down and get a good look. One was red and it had this white lacy stuff around the top, and one was yellow and black, like a bee."

Sixth grader Vicki Jordan said that it took her about thirty minutes to get used to it, and she considers that normal. "At first I was like, 'What? That's weird,' but then after a while I started to think that it was a really cool idea. I guess it was just weird at first, but then you start to get used to it, and then you think it's cool," explained Vicki.

Melodee Simon, another sixth grader, has never gotten used it. She said, "People only notice it because Stockville's a small school. If this was a bigger place, nobody would really care about Fara and her dumb socks. I actually thought people would stop caring after we graduated from elementary school."

That doesn't seem to be most people's opinion, but an interview with Fara Ross reveals that maybe she wishes it were.

"I don't really have a choice now," Fara explained. "Everybody expects me to wear these socks, so I can't let them down."

For Fara, being so well known has become stifling. This is a good example of how freedom can take a bad turn. She gets a lot of attention, and even though it is good attention she is tired of always having to think about her socks. She said that "this is the opposite of freedom" because she is always trying to please everybody and she can't really be unique. And that's what she was trying to do in the first place.

Fara remains friendly and imaginative anyway, and she still lives up to her free-thinking reputation. Everybody still looks at her feet every day, and they are never let down. But Fara wants people to look at other good things she does, and she is currently running for student council president of Stockville Middle School so that she can make a difference in more ways that matter to her.

"I never knew something so small, like socks, could play such a big part in someone's life," said Fara. "I wonder if other people feel stuck because of small things."

Maybe one day soon Fara will be able to make a difference in a way that lets people know her for something else, so she can choose her socks with freedom. Either way, Fara Ross is a real preteen role model in Stockville, socks or not.

The article ran in Wednesday's newspaper, which circulated through three towns with the afternoon mail. Jody met Fara on the corner in the morning with an advance copy, glowing. Fara made sure Jody didn't walk into any trees or garbage pails while she read the article and byline aloud as many times as she could before they reached the school (three and a half).

On Wednesday evening her mother knocked gently on her door and said, "Fara, hon, I had no idea," and her father tiptoed into her room while she was finishing up homework and silently replaced her sock-shaped lamp with a regular one.

On Thursday she wore a glittery ankle-length sock and a pale blue sock with clouds on it, and everybody whispered and pointed like they did on the very first day of her statement. Jody grinned at her, and soccer-player-Neil gave her a thumbs-up. Mr. Z. saluted her in the hallway, and her English teacher gave her a sympathetic smile, which was the most emotion Fara had seen on her stonelike face all year. "Funny," Fara wrote in her journal that night. "This is kind of fun again."

On Friday and all weekend she listened to Jody repeat the compliments she'd received on her article from Gary Ho-something, and she thought about the difference that sharing her story had possibly made. And she mixed her socks with new enthusiasm.

On the following Wednesday the letters started coming.

13. Fame

THE LETTERS FIRST APPEARED IN THE LETTERS to the Editor section. "To the editor of the *Stockville Weekly Reporter*," they'd begin.

"Jody Gower's well-written exposé regarding Fara Ross's footwear conundrum was engaging and insightful. It was refreshing to see that today's youth are interested in making a difference in whatever small ways they can. The Young Journalist did an admirable job of depicting the intricacies and inherent paradoxes of freedom of expression and individuality."

Or "Jody Gower's article was a pleasure to read. That Young Journalist is certainly headed somewhere! I am proud to say that both young women are real preteen role models in Stockville, 'socks or not.'"

Or "Thank you for printing 'When Freedom Isn't Freedom.'

It was wonderful reading about today's young people and issues that do not involve 'wrapping music' or 'hop hop' or whatever it is today's puzzling generation thinks about."

Or, in one particular case: "With all due respect to a certain 'Young Journalist,' it is not fair that a certain young woman have an entire article dedicated to her in a town newspaper when she is running for student council. This publicity places the other candidate, Melodee Simon, at a disadvantage, even though this other candidate, Melodee Simon, is just as worthy of having articles written about her. If you are not prepared to have long articles about both student council candidates, namely Melodee Simon, you shouldn't have any at all. Sincerely, Ms. Linda Simon."

So many letters came in that week that Gary Ho-something couldn't print them all. He handed all the extras to Jody in a hefty pile, the rubber band stretched so taut that it snapped before she got home. Also in the stack were letters not to the editor, but to Fara and Jody themselves. These letters began "Dear Jody" or "Dear Fara," or—their favorite—"Dear Miss Gower" or "Dear Miss Ross," which caused them to giggle happily and picture themselves reading the letters while wearing business suits, with briefcases at their sides. ("Secretary," Jody would say in a husky voice, "please take down my response to this letter while I dictate, and then place it in my attaché case so I can sign it later.") "I think you should keep wearing mismatched socks," these letters would say.

Or "Stop wearing different socks if it is consuming your life."

Or "Don't worry about what others think. You are you and they are not."

Sometimes people wrote that they understood perfectly because they, too, hated socks. "Socks are too conventional," they'd say, or "Socks are too smelly after you wear them."

Fara found these, the letters of agreement, to be the most interesting. "I wore thin socks when I tried on my shoes at the store, and now all the rest of my socks are thicker, so my shoes are too tight," someone complained. "I hate socks too because they always slide down and I get blisters right below my ankles," a boy's letter read. A girl wrote that her aunt took up drawing on socks with puffy paints and now forces her to wear them to show off her talent. A mother shared Fara's anger because she has to walk and feed the family dog, named Socks, because her children didn't live up to their promises to do so.

After reading a letter aloud, the girls would place it in a shoe box with socks drawn on the sides. Jody would raise her eyebrows and Fara would nod, her brain in overdrive. It seemed everyone had a sock sob story and was eager to share.

And then they started getting letters from people who

hated other things: eyeglasses, French braids, tea bags. An old woman who let her dislike of soap operas ruin her every afternoon; a businessman whose whole day could be soured by the newsprint that rubbed off on his fingers in the morning; a boy who couldn't stand toothpaste because he couldn't help but swallow it and then feel like throwing up.

Fara sat cross-legged on her bed on Wednesday afternoon, one red sock and one green sock poking out from beneath her, her journal on her lap, and numerous sock letters sprawled on her bedspread. Now that her statement and its negative effects were known throughout the town, how did it all add up?

She wrote: "1. I made a difference in my own life by making my socks fun again."

That was true. And making a difference in her own life was better than nothing. But of course it wasn't enough. Because making a difference in her own life didn't take too much, she reasoned. After all, she could do that by parting her hair differently or sleeping with her head at the opposite end of the bed. She pondered both of those things for a moment but then decided she liked her hair the way it was, and she didn't feel like untucking and retucking her sheets. More importantly, she didn't want to become known for anything else just yet.

Then she wrote: "2. The publicity will help me win the

FAME

election, and then I can make an even bigger difference."

This one was certainly true. It was the reason Fara had started making this list instead of focusing on her homework, and now it was the reason she couldn't concentrate on the list enough to add anything else. For among the sock letters surrounding her was a letter that Mrs. Henderson had handed her during social studies while everybody whispered, a thin piece of paper folded in half with a concise message typed on it:

To: Students Running for Student Council President
    and Their Campaign Managers
From: Mr. Zolitski
Please report to my room tomorrow immediately
following eighth period for a brief but mandatory
meeting.

14. The Problem with Outside Publicity

WHEN FARA AND JODY ENTERED MR. Z.'S ROOM, the ponytailed student council adviser was sitting on his chair, with nothing on his desk (not his bare feet, nor his patch-covered backpack) except for a small stack of papers and his folded hands. His thumbs—one with a black and silver ring on it—tapped each other slowly. Melodee Simon was already sitting right next to Mr. Z. in the circle of student desks, one leg crossed over the other under a pink skirt, her feet in what she made sure everyone knew were three-hundred-dollar boots. When she saw Fara, she huffed audibly and stared at Mr. Z., and Fara could see that she was trying very hard not to look at her or say anything.

Mr. Z. smiled at the girls and checked his watch. "We're just waiting for Melodee's campaign manager . . . and here she is. Rad."

Zoë Wilson entered, announced by the recognizable chink of the dozens of safety pins that lined the straps of her backpack. She sat down, leaving an empty seat between her and Melodee. Fara watched her in disbelief. When all of the candidates and their campaign managers had met last week to go over the rules of the election, Melodee didn't have a manager yet. Fara expected someone to step up and help her for the extra credit, but she was shocked to see Zoë, who was quirky but cool and generally well liked. Jody slid a piece of paper onto Fara's lap: "Maybe Mr. Z. made her because no one else would do it?" Fara nodded. That probably explained it.

Mr. Z. clapped his hands. "So, there's been a lot of controversy in this election so far," he said, "which is pretty amazing, considering the campaign period hasn't even started yet."

The door opened and everybody's head turned toward it at once. Joe Mescala stood in the doorway, red-faced but grinning, as though he'd just completed the mile run but had beaten the school record. Soccer-player-Neil's forehead was just barely visible behind Joe, and his arm was outstretched, his hand curled around a strap on Joe's book bag. "Sorry we're late," said Joe.

Mr. Z. adjusted himself as though he wasn't used to sitting in chairs and didn't know how to be comfortable in them. "This meeting is only for presidential candidates, guys."

Joe nodded dumbly but didn't move from the doorway. "Neil's running for vice president."

Mr. Z. crossed his arms. "Exactly," he said.

"So vice president doesn't count as presidential? Even though it has the word 'president' in it?"

Melodee snorted and crossed her arms.

"Just wanted to make sure," said Neil quickly. "Let's go," he hissed to Joe.

But Joe remained poker-faced. "Well, since we're here, we might as well stay, right? I mean, this could be important information."

Mr. Z. didn't even crack a smile. "It doesn't concern you. Good-bye, guys."

Fara could hear Joe say, "Nothing wrong in trying, man," and the sound of someone falling against a locker after Mr. Z. had closed the door.

Mr. Z. shook his head and picked up right where he'd left off. "Controversy," he said. "And yeah, all of this scandal makes it really feel like politics"—he stood up, walked around to the front of his desk, and sat down on it—"but you all know the main rule: This is a friendly election. What does that mean exactly? Well, I told all of you and your campaign teams when you first signed up that you can only say positive things about yourself and say nothing negative about other candidates. And you can spend only fifteen dollars on posters and other campaign stuff. But now parents"—Fara could have sworn she saw him glance at Melodee—"have been calling about outside publicity, and the truth is we don't really have a rule about that."

Fara looked down. She heard Jody take a quick breath.

Mr. Z. continued, "It's never been an issue before."

"I don't know," Zoë cut in. "'Neil is hot' is written on the wall in the girls' bathroom on the second floor. That could be considered outside publicity, right? But the vice presidential people don't have to be here."

"We're not talking about stuff like that," Melodee said, glaring at her campaign manager. "I mean, my name is written on a desk somewhere."

Fara glanced at Jody and resisted rolling her eyes. If Melodee's name was written on a desk and it said anything that wouldn't make her cry, she probably wrote it herself.

"Then I guess you're both even," said Zoë.

"What?" shouted Melodee. "I'm not running against Neil; I'm running against Fara. And we are not even. No way! Fara's name was in the newspaper!"

"To be fair," said Zoë easily, "your name was mentioned in the article too. And then it was mentioned in a letter to the editor yesterday."

Melodee made a face that resembled that of an angry poodle. "That is *not* the same," she said through clenched pink braces.

"Okay, okay," Mr. Z. cut in. "This is a friendly election; remember how we just went over that?"

Zoë smiled and popped a piece of gum into her mouth.

"My orthodontist says you shouldn't chew gum with braces," Melodee said.

"Thank you, Melodee," Zoë said sincerely. "That's good advice." She continued to chew.

"Mr. Z.—," Melodee started.

"I can't make Zoë stop chewing gum."

Jody giggled.

Melodee started to stand up. "Mr. Z.—"

"I'm taking care of it."

"But, Mr. Z.—"

"Melodee. Zoë. Fara and Jody." Mr. Z. ran his fingers through his ponytail. Now he had everyone's attention. "No more outside publicity, all right?"

They all nodded. Mr. Z. looked directly at Jody, and she nodded again.

"We can't take back what's already been done, but from now on, you can spend the fifteen dollars on materials for your posters, and that's it for advertising. Speaking of which, all of your posters seem good to go. You can start putting them up tomorrow after school so they'll be up when everyone comes in Monday morning."

Melodee humphed. "I think there should have to be a Preteen Spotlight about *me* in the *Stockville Weekly Reporter*," she mumbled.

Mr. Z. sighed and glanced at the clock. "You guys are going to make me late for tai chi," he said. "Melodee, I understand your concern, but let's face it: The article ran a week ago, and campaigning doesn't start until Monday. The speeches and election aren't until three weeks from Monday. By that time the article will have been published a month ago, and not many sixth graders are going to remember it and use it to make their decision. Fara, you are not allowed to mention the article in your speech or any of your other campaign materials, okay?" As he said it, he turned toward her and gave a small wink.

Fara nodded.

Mr. Z. turned back to Melodee. "She's not going to mention it, so there you go."

No one moved or said anything.

"Go ahead," Mr. Z. said. "Thank you for coming. See you kids tomorrow."

Well, that wasn't so bad, Fara thought as she stood up and put on her backpack. She could tell by the look on Jody's face that she agreed.

"Fara," Mr. Z. said. "Let me talk to you for a second. You, too, Jody."

Fara's chest started tingling. *Uh-oh,* she thought. *Here it comes.*

Zoë had already left, but Melodee heard it and smiled sweetly at Fara as she and her overpriced boots marched out of the room.

The girls approached Mr. Z.'s desk. He waited a few moments and then glanced outside the door. "Jody, that article was very well written," he said. "Great job."

Jody's eyes widened. "Um, thank you," she said. Then she looked at Fara and burst into a grin.

"And Fara," he continued, motioning toward her socks, "you've got the right idea. Hang in there, kiddo."

15. Caroline's Quiet Idea

"AND THEN HE TOLD ME THAT MY ARTICLE WAS really well written, and he told Fara to hang in there!" Jody gushed to Vicki while pressing a Vote for Fara and School Won't Sock poster onto the wall.

"Cool," Vicki said, placing a folded piece of tape on the back of the next poster. "He must hate Melodee like everyone else." She pulled another length of masking tape and ripped it with her teeth.

"You really think so?" said Caroline from across the hall, her face hidden behind a "Don't Sock . . . Vote for Fara" poster. She carefully ripped a three-inch piece of masking tape and wound it around her small finger, sticky side out.

Vicki rolled her eyes. "Come on. You don't like Melodee, do you, Caroline?"

"Well, no, but—"

"See? No one does. I think it's safe to say Mr. Z. doesn't either. And what he said in the meeting just proves it."

Fara picked up the stack of posters and a roll of tape. "But did you tell them what's even cooler?" she asked Jody.

Jody looked at her.

"The letters . . . ," Fara said.

"I saw the letters in the paper," Vicki said.

"No, there are more."

"More?" asked Caroline. She stepped back to make sure she had hung a poster evenly.

Jody nodded, her curls bouncing wildly. "Yeah, there were some that didn't go in the newspaper because they were written directly to me or Fara. Not, like, written directly to us like to our houses, because they didn't know our addresses, but directly like the letters say 'Dear Jody.'"

"What do they say?" asked Phillip, who was watching from against the wall, since Vicki had pointed out that every poster he'd hung was crooked.

"Some say they really liked the article," said Jody excitedly. Then she paused a second and turned away to put up a poster, her face turning slightly pink.

Fara nodded. "And some say that they also hate socks for various reasons. I never realized so many people hate socks."

"But why would people hate *socks*?" asked Phillip, his voice squeaking on the last word. Vicki snickered. Phillip cleared his throat, scratched his head, and added, "I mean, besides you, Fara."

"A lot of reasons," she responded with a shrug. "One woman hates them because she thinks they make her feet look fat."

"But that's not the socks' fault," Phillip said.

"It's her fat feet's fault," said Vicki.

Phillip continued, "Why do they let it bother them so much?"

Fara pressed a poster to the wall. "I guess because they just never talk about it? If you don't tell anyone, who can you take it out on but the socks themselves?" She giggled then, picturing pairs of socks with minds of their own, reading books and eating popcorn. Then she stopped when she realized that even in her head the pairs didn't match. "Like, I felt so much better after finally talking to Jody."

Vicki snorted. "Yeah, but yours is a big thing. No offense, but those sound pretty stupid."

"Some are bigger," Jody put in. "Like this girl from the high school whose aunt makes her wear ugly socks."

Vicki rolled her eyes. "Yeah, that sounds big."

Fara crossed her arms to contain her rising anger.

"Sometimes a small thing feels big when you can't do anything about it."

"Well," Caroline said with a tiny shrug and a blink of her eyes, "why don't they do something about it, then?"

16. Sock Haters Unite

"I AM GOING TO HAND BACK YOUR QUIZZES on the events leading up to the American Revolution," Mrs. Henderson said. "But first, can someone please tell me, what was the Quartering Act?"

Joe Mescala raised his hand. "That was the tax on quarters," he said confidently.

Mrs. Henderson sighed and patted Joe on the head. Everyone giggled. "I wouldn't laugh if I were you," she said. "I can't even tell you how many of you got that one wrong. The Quartering Act said that Americans had to house British soldiers in their homes. They had to provide them with *living quarters*. They did not have quarter coins in the 1770s."

"Then, what did they put in pay phones?" Joe asked. A few people snickered.

"That's a silly question," Mrs. Henderson replied. "The colonists all had cell phones."

The whole class laughed, though many people stopped once they received their quiz back. Fara got a 95 on it—apart from mixing up the dates of the Quebec Act and the Stamp Act, she had known the American colonists' complaints inside and out. She looked at the long list of grievances. The Townshend Acts, the Intolerable Acts . . . so many people were angry about the same things. With all of the letters she and Jody had received since the article had come out a week before, she could construct a list just as long, made up entirely of sock problems. Maybe socks weren't as important as all of these acts—it's not like there was a sock tax—but Caroline was right: A long list of grievances like that just couldn't be ignored. In fact, it went against everything the founding fathers stood for!

"So," said Mrs. Henderson. "With all of these complaints the colonists had against the British government—this long list that you had to fill in on your quiz—the colonists knew it was time to do something about it."

Fara sat up straight and listened intently. It was time to do something about the list of sock complaints too.

"They needed to get organized," Mrs. Henderson continued. "They needed to meet together to discuss the issues and, together, come up with a solution. So in 1774 representatives from twelve of the colonies met in Philadelphia to hold the First Continental Congress."

It all clicked in Fara's brain. That was it.

The moment the bell rang, Fara sprinted out of the room, leaped up the stairs, and waited impatiently at Jody's locker. When Jody finally arrived, Fara put her hands on her friend's shoulders. "Guess what?" she said. "Guess *what*?"

"Tell me!" urged Jody.

"The letters," Fara started. "That keep coming. Think about the Continental Congress, right?"

Jody shook her head rapidly. She was not expecting all of the excitement to be about social studies. "The Continental Congress? Slow down, Fars. Don't die."

Fara grinned and took a few breaths to gather her thoughts. "People keep writing to us because no one realized that there is someone else out there whose life is controlled by socks," she said slowly.

"You didn't even know until you started getting the letters," agreed Jody.

"Right. So, what if everybody knew that there are so many people out there who hate socks for whatever reason?" She saw that Jody was starting to catch on. "The letters to the editor help. But imagine if we just got everybody together in one room in Philadelphia."

"Philadelphia?"

"Or Stockville."

"Okay . . . would that help everybody, though? Just seeing that they're not alone?"

Fara leaned against the lockers. "I bet it will a little," she said. "And once we have everybody together, we can get organized and figure out what we can do about it."

"Like the Continental Congress?" Jody asked hesitantly.

"Exactly," Fara said. She clapped her hands. "We all have a common enemy. Only it's not taxation without representation; it's socks."

"So you can all do something about it together."

"Yup!"

Jody grinned. "So all they need is a leader."

Fara grinned back. "Can I come over?"

Fara and Jody entered Jody's house and dropped their jackets on the jacket chair, which always made Fara smile. In her own house coats were kept hidden in the coat closet, but in Jody's house a tall armchair was kept hidden by dozens of coats, even in the summertime. Fara had been spending heaps of time in Jody's house since kindergarten, and she didn't even know what the chair itself looked like. She figured it had to be ugly, probably so ugly that Jody's parents had made the conscious decision to keep it covered with jackets.

Dean, the youngest of the five Gower children, crawled up to the girls and woofed. Then he sat on his feet, bent his hands in front of his chest, and panted with his tongue out.

"Hi, Dean," Fara said.

"Woof," said Dean.

"You didn't tell me you got a dog."

Jody shrugged. "He's been pretending to be a dog for a few days. My mom says let him be a dog if he wants to be a dog, because if he's crawling, then at least his dirty feet aren't on the carpet."

Fara laughed. "Good boy," she said, patting Dean's mop-like curls.

"Don't encourage him," Jody said. "He already won't eat unless my mom puts his plate on the floor. Come on, let's go to my room."

Jody shared a room with her nine-year-old sister Lucy, who was sitting at her desk writing on a sheet of loose-leaf paper. When she saw Fara come in, she gasped. "Fara!" she said.

"Hi, Lucy," Fara answered.

"You're famous," Lucy said, her eyes gliding downward from Fara's face to her white sock and pink sock.

Jody crossed her arms. "What's wrong with you?" she said. "Fara comes over here all the time."

"But she was never famous before."

"Yes, she was. She's been famous since last year, dummy."

"Not *this* famous. She had a whole article about her in the newspaper."

"I know, stupid. I wrote it."

"I can't wait to tell my friends that you were here," Lucy said to Fara's feet.

Jody grunted. "Then you should go downstairs and call them right now. We have work to do."

"I'm doing work too. I'm putting my spelling words into sentences. Like this," she said, "'Enough.' My sister Jody doesn't shower enough."

Jody turned her head toward the door. "Mom!"

"Or this one," Lucy continued. "'Horrified.' A monster looked at Jody and he was horrified."

"Mom!" Jody bellowed.

"I'm right here, Jody," Mrs. Gower said from the doorway, her hands hovering over her ears. "That's not very nice, Lucy. For that you can go work on your homework downstairs and let Fara and your sister do their work up here."

Fara saw Lucy scribble "1 white 1 pink" on the top of her spelling list before packing up her notebook and heading downstairs.

Mrs. Gower smiled at Fara. "Well! As if having one famous young woman in the house wasn't enough. How are you, Miss Freedom Fighter?"

Fara felt herself blush. "I'm fine, Mrs. Gower."

"Still keeping up with the mismatched socks, I see?"

"For now. Yeah."

"Well, you two are quite the talk of town, you know. I heard two little old ladies talking about you over the cantaloupes in the supermarket today. I'm very proud of both of you, and I'm sure your mother is too."

Fara nodded.

Mrs. Gower turned to her daughter. "Now if only you could speak to your sister as nicely as you write for the newspaper."

Jody bent her head from side to side as if to say, *Yeah, yeah, yeah.*

"When are you going to have another article in there, Jode? Grandpa wants to know so he can tell everybody in his Scrabble club."

"Soon. Maybe even next week."

"What are you going to write about?"

"I don't know yet, Mom."

"The bad thing about writing such a fabulous first article is your second one has to live up to it. But I'm sure you'll think of something great. Maybe one of your other friends has trouble with shoelaces."

Fara chuckled. Jody stared.

"I haven't heard very much of the cello this week," Mrs. Gower said with a nod toward the large case in the corner.

"Boris will not be pleased tomorrow night."

Jody snorted. "Boris will never be pleased."

Fara was used to hearing about Jody's cello teacher, a large, hairy man named Boris who said little in English besides, "You need practice." Even when Jody did practice, Boris insisted that she needed more. Fara had never met him, but she knew that Jody was always happiest right after her Thursday-night cello lesson, as that meant it was the longest period of time possible before Boris would be at her house again.

"Boris is a good teacher," said Mrs. Gower. "Imagine how much you'd be learning if you practiced once in a while."

"Okay, Mom," said Jody.

"Those lessons are expensive—"

"I'll practice, Mom," Jody said.

"Boris travels a long way to teach you—"

"I know, Mom," Jody said forcefully.

"All right," said Mrs. Gower. "I get it; I'll let you girls do your work. Stay for dinner if you'd like, Fara. Steak and baked potatoes. I'm trying to make food that's hard to eat without your hands or utensils so maybe Dean will decide he wants to sit at the table and stop barking."

When Mrs. Gower left, Fara sat on the desk chair and Jody climbed into her bottom bunk bed. She'd had the top bunk until about two years ago, when she begrudgingly

switched as a seventh birthday gift for Lucy. Lucy had origi-
nally promised in return that Jody could sit up there twice a
week and sleep up there once a month, but she took those
privileges back as her eighth birthday present. ("You're
supposed to get *more* generous as you grow up," Jody had
grumbled.)

"So do you think we should get everybody together?" Fara
asked, getting right down to it.

"Sure. Like the Continental Congress, right?"

Fara laughed. "Yeah."

"The First Sockinental Congress. And then I could write
an article covering it for the *Weekly Reporter!*"

Fara started to get excited, until she remembered that
if she was the subject of any more outside publicity, she'd
probably be disqualified from the election. From the way
Jody was biting her lower lip, Fara figured she probably
remembered as well.

"How can we advertise it without giving you any outside
publicity that Melodee and her mom could complain about?"
Jody mumbled.

Fara thought. The newspaper would be the most conve-
nient. Just put a small ad or have Jody write a short article
saying the time and place. Or posters. She knew her mother
would be excited to help her make posters for anything, and
so would Phillip (probably so excited that he'd trip over the

phone cord after she asked him). It didn't seem fair that she couldn't advertise for something completely unrelated to her campaign because it would give her "outside publicity." She didn't *ask* for everybody to associate anything involving socks with her and the presidency. The presidency was supposed to be about doing something that didn't involve socks.

The silence was suddenly broken by Lucy dancing in, twisting and leaping like the world's clumsiest ballerina. "Stop it, Luce," Jody shouted. "You don't even take ballet. You just look like an idiot."

"Who cares if I take ballet? I know how to *dahnce*!" Lucy said, twirling into the bedpost. She continued spinning, calling out "First position" and some made-up French terms like "Roundazay" and "Spin-e-mwah." After barely landing a leap, she stuck one leg in the air and reached down to pick up a letter from the box by Jody's leg. "What's this?" she asked, nearly collapsing.

"Put it down," Jody growled.

"A letter?"

"It's not yours."

"'Dear Miss Gower,'" she read in a squeaky voice. "'I lo-o-o-ved your article.'"

Jody lunged after Lucy, who spun away just in time to save herself but not the letter. With a loud "Give it to me!"

and an even louder "Get away!" the paper ripped right down the center.

Fara sat perfectly still in the desk chair, pretending she was invisible.

Jody's feet remained planted, but her teeth were clenched. One of her hands slowly stiffened into a fist, and the other tightened around the side of the bunk bed ladder to keep herself from physically attacking her sister. "Look what you did!" she screeched.

"Look what *I* did?" Lucy asked with half the fervor. "It's your own fault. Look, you ripped it right through the address on top. Now how are you going to write back?"

Jody froze midpounce. Her eyes lit up. She twisted over to look at Fara, who still wasn't quite sure she wanted her presence to be acknowledged. "That's it!" Jody said. "It's so simple. We'll just write back to all the people we want to come, telling them about the meeting. That can't be considered outside publicity because Mr. Z. and Melodee won't even find out about it."

Fara started to smile. Why didn't she think of that? It made so much sense. Nobody could get them in trouble for writing a letter to someone who had written them a letter first, right?

"Lucy, you're good for something after all!" Jody said, moving toward her sister. Lucy winced, unsure if this was a trick to tackle her or not. But Jody reached out and pulled her into a tight hug; she even kissed her on the forehead with a loud "Mwah!" The expression on Lucy's face made Fara crack up laughing—you would think it was a giant, slimy spider hugging her instead of her older sister. "Isn't my sister the best?" Jody said to Fara while patting Lucy's back. "Thank you, Lucy Diane Gower!" she sang while she took the two pieces of the letter from Lucy's limp fingers and returned them to the box. The second Jody's arms were off, Lucy bolted. Jody exploded with laughter. "Jody: one. Lucy: zero."

17. Sock-rilege

"I GOT YOUR LETTER," PHILLIP SAID TO FARA
and Jody on their way to the cafeteria the next week. They
had thought it would be funny to write him a sock response
letter and had mailed it with the rest. "And I would be honored to attend the First Sockinental Congress on Thursday
night," he said in a formal voice.

"Splendid," replied Fara in the same tone.

"Wait," said Jody. "Thursday night?"

"Yeah . . . at least, I think that's what the letter said,"
Phillip said. "I've been practicing that response all day."

"I thought we were doing it on Friday," Jody said to Fara.

Fara shook her head. "I forgot to tell you. The party room
at Lane's Lanes isn't free on Friday, so my dad suggested
Thursday at seven o'clock instead. I changed all the letters.
I didn't think it would make a difference."

"Fara!" cried Jody. "Boris!"

"Boris?" said Phillip.

Fara's face fell. She remembered the instant Jody said it. Of course Jody couldn't come on Thursday night. "I'm so sorry, Jode. I should have checked with you before I mailed the letters."

"Checked?" Jody said.

"No, I should have known. I don't know what I was thinking."

"I can't believe you forgot. I only complain to you about Boris every single week."

"What's a boris?" asked Phillip.

"A big, hairy cello teacher," muttered Jody. "Who is very expensive and travels a long way to teach me." She threw her backpack down and dropped into a chair at their usual table.

Fara felt terrible. Her mistake was huge. Sock-rilegious. "I can write everybody and change it," she suggested.

"Forget it," said Jody. "It's too late."

Fara wanted to insist that it wasn't, but she knew that it was. "I'm so, so, so sorry. I'll call you right after the meeting and tell you everything. I promise. It'll be just like you were there."

Jody sighed. "This socks," she said.

18. The First Sockinental Congress

THE FIRST SOCKINENTAL CONGRESS CONVENED
in the party room of Lane's Lanes bowling alley at seven
o'clock Thursday night. Members sat behind tables pushed
into an awkward U. They sported name tags in the shape
of a sock even though Fara had repeatedly pointed out
to her mother, who designed them, that everybody there
hated socks. Fara sat in the open part of the U behind a
table covered with a bowling tablecloth. She was so nervous even her feet were sweating in her black sock and
tie-dyed sock. Her parents stood in the back. She had
begged for them to stay outside, but now that she was
facing a room of strangers who were quietly mingling and
munching on food from the snack counter, she was glad
for their presence. She was not glad that Phillip's father
was there, giving her a thumbs-up every few minutes from

behind an oversize video camera, but some things couldn't be avoided.

Phillip waved at her from his spot at the edge of the U. He motioned for Fara to use the gavel he'd brought her just for the occasion. She motioned back that she'd start in a minute. She stepped outside the party room and walked to the bathroom to splash some water on her face. She looked at her watch. Jody was probably sitting down with Boris right now. Rubbing her eyes with the palms of her hands, Fara thought back to second grade, when her teacher was so impressed with an entry in Fara's journal about helping her parents run a clothing drive that she asked her to read it aloud during parents' night. Even though Fara had read the short paragraph aloud at home from the top of the stairs with enough volume and passion to stir her imagined audience of thousands, the moment she got up in front of her eighteen classmates and their parents, she seemed to forget how to move her lips. Her parents smiled and urged her on, and her teacher said she could sit down if she wanted to and maybe try again a little later. Fara was about to close her journal and cry, when she looked to Jody, who was sitting at her desk all the way by the door and making faces. Fara could still remember the exact faces Jody made. First she stuck her hand under her chin and waved, and she stuck her tongue through the large gap where she had lost her front teeth.

Then she took a ruler from her desk and balanced it on her upper lip to make it look like a long, straight mustache. Then she puffed up her cheeks and used her hands to push her ears forward, making a hilariously convincing monkey face. When Fara started to giggle, Jody scratched her head and under her armpit and even let out a soft "Ooh-ooh-aah-aah!" Fara laughed so hard she shook, and Jody got in trouble with both her parents and her teacher, but once Fara stopped laughing, she was able to read her paragraph aloud as though she was just speaking to Jody. After that Fara had delivered countless book reports and presentations without a single butterfly in her stomach. Yet now she was scared silly to get up in front of the First Sockinental Congress.

She looked in the mirror, ran her fingers through her hair, and headed back toward the party room.

"F Dawg," said the young man working the front desk. He held out his hand for Fara to slap.

"Hi, Benny," she said.

"Has your meeting started yet?"

"In a few minutes."

"All right," he said, unbuttoning his Lane's Lanes shirt to reveal an "I'm with Stupid" T-shirt underneath. "Hey," he called to a worker who was dusting video game machines. "Come work the desk. I'm going on break. I always lose socks in the dryer. I want to see if this'll do me any good."

From Benny's laugh Fara figured out that her face must have expressed her awkward combination of confusion and nerves.

"Your meeting?" Benny said. "That's where I can go complain about my sock problems, right?"

"What's that?" asked a familiar voice from the counter. It was Zoë. "Hey, Fara," she said. "What's this meeting?"

Benny patted Fara on the shoulder. "See you in there, F Dawg," he said.

"Can I come to the meeting?" Zoë asked, popping her gum. She was standing with a group of older boys, all of whom were either pierced or tattooed, or both. She pointed to one wearing a shirt with a skull and crossbones on it. He was demonstrating some karate moves on one of the others. "That's my brother," she said. "I was going to go bowling with him and his friends, but I'd much rather go to a sock meeting."

She wasn't Jody, but she was a familiar face. And Fara could definitely use one more of those in there. But the reason she and Jody had written letters back was to avoid having Melodee or her campaign team find out about the meeting. . . .

"I won't tell Melodee. Or Mr. Z. I promise."

Fara was convinced. "Come on," she said.

"Yes!" hissed Zoë. She told her brother to start bowling without her.

As they walked to the party room, Fara filled her in on how she'd received letters and written letters back. "But now I've got all these people here," she said, "and I don't really know what to do with them."

Zoë laughed. "It sounds like they're all itching to share. I bet all you have to do is get them started."

Fara blinked. She hadn't thought about it that way. She entered the room and sat down in her head chair. Phillip applauded but then quickly stopped himself. Mrs. Ross rushed up to Zoë and got her name so she could make her a name tag. Instead of sitting by Phillip, the newly name-tagged Zoë pulled up a chair and sat next to Fara.

"Hi, everyone," said Fara as confidently as she could.

"Hello," said a gangly teenage boy whose name tag read TIM.

Everybody giggled. So did Fara. She introduced herself. Then she introduced Zoë and Phillip. She thanked every-one for coming. "After the article in the *Weekly Reporter*," she said, "I got so many letters—from all of you, but even more—from people who said that they also had problems with socks. And it made me feel better to read them, because I knew at least I wasn't the only one. So I figured that if I got all of you together, then you'd all see that you're not the only one, and you'd feel better too. Or maybe we could even figure out ways to help each other."

Phillip started to applaud. Zoë laughed.

"So," Fara continued with a glance toward Zoë, "you could just all share with each other. But maybe someone wants to start by sharing with everyone? You already know why I'm fed up with socks. But it'd be cool for me to put faces with sock stories. So does someone else want to go?"

"I volunteer," said Tim without a moment's hesitation. He stood up. "I'm Tim, as you all can see from my name tag—which is really cool, by the way." He motioned to Fara's mother, who shrugged politely and then shot Fara a look that said, *So there.* Tim continued, "A long time ago—at least, I think this is how the story goes—my grandpa and grandma were young and carefree." He fluttered his eyelashes for effect.

Fara giggled; she remembered Tim's letter. Zoë nudged Fara and smiled. A chubby girl with round plastic glasses let out a snort. Tim looked at her, and she turned bright red and giggled more, which only made her snort again.

"So, my young and carefree grandparents bought an apartment when they got married, but the people they bought it from were kind of messy, and it needed a lot of cleaning up. They cleaned all day and all night—that's the way my grandpa tells it. They didn't just do the usual things, like vacuum and dust, you know? They got down on their hands and knees and scrubbed the floors, and they pretty much dunked the bathroom in bleach, and my grandpa got up on a ladder to clean every little crevice of every little closet. And the very last thing they did was wax the floor in the kitchen. Once the whole place had that clean smell and shine—you know the smell I'm talking about?—they were so excited and so happy that they started to dance. And not really-old-people-type dancing, because they were young and carefree then, but wild dancing, like . . . what's the name of that dance? The baked potato or something."

"The mashed potato!" corrected an adult nearby.

Tim laughed. "Well, my grandpa likes to do everything bigger and better, so they probably did the garlic mashed potato with gravy. Anyway, they were dancing around in the kitchen in just their *socks*, really happy, dancing, dancing. . . ." He did a little shimmy, then stopped suddenly. "And *boom!* My grandpa slips in his socks—because the floor is so slippery from being waxed, remember?—and breaks his ankle." Tim paused for effect.

Phillip said, "That's it?"

"I wish," answered Tim. "But that's just where the story starts! So he broke his ankle, and he had to get a cast and crutches and everything. And it was tough because their apartment was on the sixth floor and there was no elevator. But it still healed and everything, and he's just fine today. *Except* that he blames socks for the fall. He could have blamed floor wax or cleaning or the mashed potato, but he figured that it was the socks' fault that he slipped and broke his ankle. So he started boycotting socks. He's really proud of it too; he always tells me and my sister that when he was in the hospital for the ankle, he said to my grandma, very bravely, 'I swear I will never wear socks again.' And he hasn't. Not even once. He threw away all of his socks and never bought new ones. And boy, do his feet smell! Whew! But back then he didn't only swear to never wear socks again, he made my grandma swear that she would never wear socks again either. He was just trying to look out for her, I guess. But to this day he still thinks socks are involved in an evil plot to destroy the human race. So he still boycotts socks, and—this is the worst part, apart from his smelly feet— he doesn't want me or my sister to wear socks! Any socks! Ever!"

Phillip gasped.

"Like"—Tim caught his breath and continued—"my dad lets us wear socks. He had enough of not wearing them when he grew up. But he knows how seriously my grandpa takes his no-socks rule, so whenever my grandpa would come over, the socks would have to go. Seriously, my dad would warn us, and we'd all put our socks in a shoe box and hide it in the base- ment! It's ridiculous. And a few months ago my grandpa came to live with us. So I can't wear socks ever. He won't listen to any reason. He doesn't care that if the socks are in shoes they can't cause any harm. So the past few months I've gotten so many blisters, and my shoes smell like the goat pen at the petting zoo. Sometimes I sneak around and tell friends to bring extra socks to school or wherever for me, but then I have to remember to hide them when I get home. I don't know what to do. And that's why I came to the First Sockinental Congress." He shrugged. "Thank you." He sat down.

Phillip applauded, and this time everyone else joined in, so he looked at Fara and beamed. She smiled back, though her heart was pounding. That was a great story, and Tim had told it with gusto, but what if no one had any way to help him?

The girl who had snorted before raised her hand meekly. "I might be able to help you," she said.

Fara was so excited she had to restrain herself from jumping up and down. But she did find and squeeze Zoë's hand under the table.

"My name is Sandra," the girl continued, "and my aunt— well, she's sort of my aunt—well, anyway, she has this ridiculous business idea that she thinks will work. She buys really cheap socks and then draws stuff on them with puffy paints. Music notes, smiley faces, balloons, you know. So they're really ugly. I mean *really* ugly. But for some reason she doesn't think so, and she thinks that people will buy them.

She insists—*insists*—that I wear them to kind of show them off and get people interested, at least until her sales pick up. But they're so ugly."

Fara gave Sandra a half smile. "I remember her letter," she whispered to Zoë. "I felt so bad because she said she gets made fun of for wearing those ugly socks. But how ugly could they be?"

"Here, look for yourselves," Sandra said, as though Fara had spoken to her and not to Zoë. She lifted the bottoms of her jeans. Her thin white sock was covered in neon symbols—curlicues, arrows, question marks, stars.

Fara wrinkled her nose.

"Well, those are . . . different," whispered Zoë. Fara covered her mouth so Sandra wouldn't see her giggling.

Sandra sighed and let her jeans fall. "I know," she said. "They're terrible." But then she brightened and explained that her aunt had once made a mistake and painted on the bottoms of the socks, and it made the bottoms so sticky that she could hardly walk on the linoleum in her kitchen in them. "We threw that pair out, but I'm sure she could make you a few pairs of those, Tim," Sandra said excitedly, "and your grandpa would see that there's no way you could slip in them! And then that'd be a start toward wearing other socks."

"And then your feet won't smell," said Phillip as though he had just solved the riddle of the century.

"All right!" said Tim.

"I think I might know a way to help *you*, Sandra," said Zoë.

The room began to buzz. Everyone was eager to share a story so that the guy in the next seat, or across the way, or standing in the back, might hold the solution in *his* story.

As everyone broke off into their own conversations, Zoë suggested that Fara wear some of Sandra's aunt's socks. "Every sock you wear gets noticed in a good way," Zoë explained, "so that might give the puffy-painted socks some good press."

"You would do that for me?" Sandra asked, visibly touched. "They're really ugly."

Fara shrugged. "Sure," she said.

After talking for another few minutes, Sandra went off to talk to Tim, who was giving a sixth-grade boy tips for keeping his sneakers smelling fresh after wearing them without socks.

"Does anyone know what to do about socks getting lost in the dryer?" shouted Benny.

"Mine do too!" called a young man from across the room. "Maybe if we put what we have left together, we can make complete pairs!"

"My mom only buys me boring white socks!" complained a girl sitting near Phillip.

"I can help you there," Fara said. "I have an entire set of drawers full of funky socks."

"My pants are a little too short, so I always have to be sure I'm wearing matching black socks, because they show when I'm walking or sitting at work," said Phillip's dad.

"I can lower the hems of your pants," said Fara's mom.

"My socks are too low!" said someone from a corner.

"Perfect—my socks are too long!" someone responded.

"I have Mr. Ranaldi for social studies!" someone said.

"I had him two years ago," someone else responded. "Does he still refer to you as 'earthlings'?"

Fara sat back and grinned. Zoë was right. All she needed to do was get them started. This was about more than socks. This was about making a difference.

"Fara," her dad said. "We need to get this room ready for a party at eight. And Benny needs to get back to work."

Fara nodded. She was going to call for everyone's attention, but instead she used Phillip's gavel. "We have to leave this room," she said. "But we could meet again."

"And give each other the socks we need to," said Tim.

"Or pants," said Phillip's dad.

"Yes, we can all exchange," said Fara. "Well, socks. Not pants."

Everybody laughed.

"A sock exchange," said Tim with a laugh. "That's awesome."

"A sock market," added Fara.

"Like the stock market?" Phillip whispered to Zoë. She nodded. He laughed.

"So same time next week, then?" Zoë said.

Fara almost confirmed that, but then she thought of Boris. "No, wait. Maybe we can do it next Friday instead."

Mr. Ross shook his head. "This room's booked, honey," he said.

"I couldn't make it on a Friday," said Tim.

"Let's keep it the same time, then," said Sandra quickly. Then she flushed and concentrated on wiping her glasses on her shirt.

Everyone mumbled in agreement and told one another how perfectly this time fit into their schedules. Fara's heart started to race. What about Boris? But there was no way she could find another time that everyone here would be able to come. "All right," she said. Maybe she could convince Mrs. Gower to let Jody skip one cello lesson. She'd beg. *I can promise to walk Dean for a whole week,* she thought with a laugh. She made a mental note to tell that to Jody later.

* * *

But by the time Jody called later that night, Fara was under the covers with the lights out. She had already rehashed the events of the First Sockinental Congress for twenty minutes with Zoë and Phillip, for fifteen with her parents, and for four pages of her journal. She was just too tired to do it again.

"Tell Jody I'm in bed," Fara said to her mother. "And that I'll tell her everything on the way to school tomorrow. I promise."

But Fara slept so soundly that she didn't wake up until her father knocked on her door and asked, "Doesn't school start in fifteen minutes?" She bolted upright and looked at her alarm clock. "Ten minutes!" she cried. She jumped out of bed, sloshed some toothpaste and water in her mouth, threw on some clothes, and put on the first two mismatched socks she could grab. As she and her father drove past Jody's block, Fara could have kicked herself. *I'll tell her everything at lunch,* Fara promised to herself.

19. Jody and Zoë

SINCE FARA WASN'T AT THE CORNER AND
didn't stop by her house on her way to school, Jody went by
her locker before homeroom. "Oh, hey, Jody," said Zoë, who
was leaning against the wall. "Have you seen Fara?"

"No, not yet."

"This is her locker, right?"

Jody nodded. "Do you want me to give her a message or
something?"

"Nah. I just wanted to tell her how cool the Sockinental
Congress was last night."

"You were there?" Jody asked.

"Yeah, it was awesome. I met some really cool people. I
can't wait to go to the sock exchange next week."

"Sock exchange?"

"Yeah, we're gonna meet up so everybody can trade socks and just hang out some more. You should come."

Jody tucked her hair behind her ears and retied her red sweatshirt around her waist. "When is it?"

"Same time," Zoë said. She took out her gum and stuck it underneath the water fountain. "Thursday at seven."

Jody crossed her arms. "Really," she said.

"Yep. How come you weren't there last night? I thought you and Fara were best friends or something."

Jody smiled tightly. "I had a cello lesson," she said.

"Oh, that socks," said Zoë with a laugh. "Well, I'm gonna go to homeroom. See you at lunch."

Jody waved dumbly and fell back against the panel of lockers. She didn't want to see Zoë at lunch, so she scribbled a note to Fara saying she was going to work on the school newspaper with Mr. Francis during fifth period. The hallway slowly emptied out except for a seventh-grade boy who was quietly panicking because he couldn't get his locker open. With less than a minute before the start of homeroom, the boy realized out loud that he was at the right locker but on the wrong floor. Jody sighed, slid the note into Fara's locker, and headed to class.

20. Ms. Linda Simon

MS. LINDA SIMON SAT UP STRAIGHT IN HER
gray and yellow suit, a string of pearls outlining her neck.
She checked her designer watch. The PTA meeting was
scheduled to begin in three minutes, but women were still
trickling in and chatting with one another. She put on a plastic smile and turned to one of the few men in the room,
Teddy Ronkel, Phillip's father.

"Hello, Teddy," she said, her voice oozing with sweetness.
"How *are* you?"

"I'm fine," he said, shaking her hand. "How are you,
Linda?"

"Oh, I'm busy. Business is booming, as usual, but that
means more work for me, of course," she said, the last word
trailing on so long it never quite ended, but rather seemed
to evaporate. She chuckled and pulled her fire red lips into

a tight smile. "And my younger daughter, Carli, just got the lead in her school play, so we've been busy practicing for that. And how is . . . Philbert?"

"Phillip is fine, thank you."

"Melodee says he is the sweetest boy. I think she wanted him on her election campaign team, but she waited too long, because he was already taken." She checked her watch again and announced for everyone to take their seats for the meeting.

"Yes," said Phillip's father. "He's helping Fara Ross."

"Oh, that's wonderful. How nice of Zach Zolitski to have made the elections into something that involves more children. Although Melodee has been taking on much of the work herself, as usual. She's such a perfectionist, that girl. Takes after her mother." She chuckled. "Is Fara involving her teammates a lot?" She sat at the head of the table and motioned for Teddy to sit next to her. "I mean, is she having a lot of meetings and such?"

He rubbed his beard. "Yes, it certainly seems to be a team effort. Although most of the meetings Phillip's been attending lately haven't been for the election, but for socks."

Ms. Simon lifted her penciled-in eyebrows. "Is that so?" she said.

*　　*　　*

After calling the meeting to a close, Ms. Linda Simon drove to Loretta's Bake Stop and bought herself a cup of coffee and a raspberry pastry to go, making sure the pastry went in a Loretta's Bake Stop bag. Coffee, pastry, and bag in hand, she continued on to Loretta and Larry Drexler's house. She rang the bell and took a large bite of the pastry before Loretta opened the door.

"Hello, Loretta," Ms. Simon sang, the sweetness of her voice rivaling that of the raspberry goop on her teeth. "How *are* you?"

Loretta smiled. "I recognize that puff pastry," she said politely. "What brings you here, Linda?"

"Mmm," she replied. Ms. Simon swallowed and washed the bite down with a sip of the coffee. "I hope it's not too late to drop by. I just wanted to speak to Larry. And when I thought of coming here, I thought of your shop and couldn't resist." She held up the bag as evidence.

Loretta let her in and called for Larry, her husband, the head of WSTV, Stockville Television. The three of them sat down at the dining-room table, and Ms. Simon proceeded to tell Larry all about a human interest story that WSTV might like to cover. "A sock market," she explained. "Right here in Stockville, headed by a young girl named Fara Ross."

"I'm not quite sure what a sock market entails," Larry

said. "But I wouldn't mind finding out. That sounds very interesting," he continued. "Just the sort of thing our viewers would enjoy."

"Really?" Ms. Simon said. "That's wonderful!" She smiled, clapped her hands, and gave him all the details.

21. Market Day

IT WAS A LOVELY THURSDAY MORNING. A
wake-up-before-the-alarm-goes-off, fifteen-minute-shower,
whole-wheat-pancakes-for-breakfast, math-homework-
finished-and-stapled, campaign-speech-typed-and-printed-
and-resting-neatly-in-a-folder-in-a-backpack morning. It
was a plaid-sock-and-checkered-sock kind of morning,
Fara decided fearlessly. One plaid and one checkered and
a striped sweater. It was just going to be that kind of day.

She arrived on Jody's porch just as Mrs. Gower was picking up the newspaper from her stoop. "Fara, dear," said Mrs.
Gower. "You missed her again."

"No way," said Fara. She looked at her striped sweater.
Maybe this day wasn't going to be quite as wonderful as she'd
thought. Fara really wanted to talk to Jody; they had barely
seen each other since last week. Fara hadn't even had a

chance to tell her the details of the sock meeting yet. She had planned on hanging out with her Saturday, but her mother dragged her out to buy her new sweaters, and Fara knew Jody wouldn't want to be submitted to that tedium. She was going to call her on Sunday for sure, but she had bumped into Zoë while helping her dad out at Lane's Lanes, and she ended up going back to Zoë's house for dinner and sock market planning. And now this was the fourth day in a row that Jody had gone to school without waiting at the corner or coming to Fara's house. At first she didn't think much of it. She had been running a little later than usual the past few days, and Jody probably had to take care of school newspaper business before homeroom. But today she'd left her house extra early to try to catch her. Jody must have left extra early as well. *Why can't she just wait for me?* Fara thought angrily.

"Is that Fara?" Lucy stepped onto the porch in her pajamas. "Hi, Fara!" she said.

"Lucy," said her mother. "Go get dressed. You're going to be late."

Lucy gave Fara a hug. "Guess what? I'm coming to the sock market tonight," she said. "With my friends."

"When Jody told us about it, Lucy was just dying to go," Mrs. Gower explained. "I hope that's all right with you?"

"It's all right, right?" asked Lucy.

Fara shrugged. "Sure," she said. "So Jody's coming too, then?" she asked excitedly.

Lucy shook her head. "Jody has cello. But don't worry, I'm coming for sure. I can't wait."

"You don't think Jody could miss just one lesson with Boris so that she could come?" Fara asked. "Maybe she can do it another day or something. If I knew how to play the cello, I'd teach her this week—"

"Sorry, Fara." Mrs. Gower told Lucy to say good-bye and gently pushed her inside to get dressed, then continued. "It's too late to change the lesson now. Boris has a strict cancellation policy. If you don't let him know forty-eight hours in advance, he charges you for it."

So why didn't Jody just ask her mom to cancel her lesson a couple days ago if she knew about the sock market? Maybe Mrs. Gower wouldn't let her, and now she was just making an excuse. Or maybe Jody only found out about it yesterday, so it was already too late. Fara hoped that Jody wasn't going to come for one of those two reasons. Something hot behind her eyes was telling her otherwise, but she forced it back. She needed to hunt down Jody during school.

Lucy jumped past the door, dressed half in school clothes and half in pajamas. "See you tonight, Fara!" she shouted.

"Yes, see you later," Mrs. Gower said.

Lucy Gower and her friends weren't the only ones who

wanted to come to the sock market. Zoë slipped Fara a note
in the hallway saying that a few of her friends were going to
come, but they promised to keep it a secret. And while mill-
ing about before gym, a group of seventh-grade boys asked if
they could come too. Fara didn't want it to get out of hand,
and she didn't want the word to spread to Melodee, but she
was so happy that she couldn't turn anyone away. As long
as she didn't bring up the election at all, it didn't count as
publicity anyway, she reasoned. And besides, what type of
freedom would she be advocating if she banned people from
attending an event based entirely around freedom?

At lunch Fara went to her usual table, but only Caroline
was there. "Where is everybody?" she asked.

"Oh, hi, Fara," Caroline said. "Phillip had to go work on
an art project he has due next week. He was almost done,
but he was bringing it home to work on it, and it flew out the
window of the bus. So now he has to start over. And Vicki's
on the lunch line."

"And Jody?" Fara asked.

"Jody's working on the school newspaper, I think. So there
are plenty of seats." Caroline smiled warmly and motioned
toward all of the empty seats. "I actually thought of a few
things to help you start the recycling program once you're
president." She blushed and motioned to the seats again. "If
you have a minute."

Fara almost sat down, but then she thought better of it. "I really don't right now," she said. "I need to go look for Jody." She started to walk purposefully out of the cafeteria, but the strictest lunch lady, the one everyone called Mean Jean, stopped her at the door. Mean Jean was a small, thin woman, but it was harder to get through her guarding the door than it would be the toughest lock.

"And where do you think you are going without a hall pass?" Jean asked. Fara did not know how such a large voice could come from such a small body. Before she could begin to respond, something hit her on the side of the head. It was a raisin.

"What was that?" Mean Jean thundered.

Fara looked to see where it had come from and saw a laughing Zoë quickly look away and munch on a sandwich.

Fara glanced at the lunch lady and hurried over to Zoë. "What are you doing?" she asked incredulously. "Starting a food fight right in front of Mean Jean?"

"Well, I had to get your attention somehow! You looked like you were on a mission, but she was not going to let you through."

"You're probably right."

"Sit down, raisin head," Zoë said. "These are my friends who are going to come to the sock market tonight. Guys, this is Fara Ross."

"The sock market sounds so cool," said one of the boys, who Fara thought was in seventh grade, or maybe even eighth. "How did you come up with the idea?"

"This is really great," Zoë said. "Fara, tell them about the meeting last week and everything. Want a raisin?"

Fara laughed. "No, thank you," she said. She sat down, opened her lunch, and started to share.

After school Fara delivered the draft of her speech to Mr. Z. Melodee was in the room having him read hers, so Fara took a seat and waited.

"I hope you didn't mention anything about socks in that speech," said Melodee in a smug voice. "Or anything that would remind people about your illegal publicity."

"Don't worry," said Fara, trying her hardest to be polite.

"Good," said Mr. Z., lifting his eyes from Melodee's speech. "This revision looks good, Miss Simon. I think I'll hold on to this copy, if that's all right."

"What?" said Melodee, who was too busy looking down her nose at Fara to listen to Mr. Z.'s request. "Um, sure," she said.

Fara stifled her laughter.

Melodee shot Fara a dirty look as she put on her designer shoulder bag. She started to leave, but then stopped and turned around as though she was remembering something.

But instead of saying anything, she glanced down at Fara's checkered and plaid socks and shook her head piteously. Then she left.

Fara handed Mr. Z. the draft of her speech. "I'm glad to say I haven't seen you in the newspaper lately," he said, scanning the page.

Fara nodded. *How strange to be congratulated for not being in the newspaper. Perhaps criminals hear that all the time from their parents,* she thought.

"A recycling program," Mr. Z. muttered as he read. "We could certainly use one of those." He got to the bottom of the page and looked up. "Good," he said. "Mind if I keep this copy?"

Fara shook her head.

"Now, just manage to keep you and your socks out of the media for a few more days, and we'll have a nice, fair election without any more complications. Right? That can't be too difficult."

"Thanks, Mr. Z.," Fara said, putting on her backpack and mentally mapping out the rest of her day. Her speech was turned in, her homework was already halfway done, and she had a sock market to prepare for.

22. Sock Market Crash

THE STOCKVILLE SOCK EXCHANGE OFFICIALLY
opened for trading at seven o'clock that evening. Phillip
masking-taped a homemade SOCK MARKET sign with a sock-
shaped arrow onto the water fountain, pointing to the party
room. Inside, Fara's and Phillip's fathers had pushed all of
the tables and chairs to the edges to accommodate a bustling
sock trading floor. A sign that read INVEST IN THE SOCK MAR-
KET, painted by Fara's mother and Phillip, hung on the far
wall. In front of it, on a card table, Fara laid out the items for
trading she had carefully selected the night before: thirty-
seven socks, her sock lamp, a set of pencils with sock-shaped
erasers, and her tie with socks on it. She had realized, with
some amusement, that she could trade away half of each
pair of socks she owned, since she never wore a set together.
But then she remembered that after the election she could

change her ways, so she kept all of her plain white ones, along with complete pairs of any others she especially liked.

Sandra's aunt set up a whole table's worth of puffy-painted socks and hung up a puffy-painted sign that said ROCKIN' SOCKS! Tim came with the intention of buying socks, and he did, in fact, make the first investment—he paid two dollars for a pair of socks Sandra had her aunt make just for him, with puffy-painted designs on the bottom to prevent slipping. Zoë announced the purchase loudly, and everyone applauded. The sock exchange had officially begun.

By 7:15 the room was packed. There was buying, selling, trading, and lots of conversation. Groups of kids Fara recognized from school stood in bunches, discussing how cool this was and offering to trade the socks on their feet for other, cooler socks. Lucy and her friends stood by Fara's table, deciding which of Fara's socks were the prettiest and then playing hand games to determine who got to buy them. Three boys from Fara's gym class sat in a corner, their sneakers by their sides, trying to calculate whose socks smelled the worst. Benny and some others were happily combining and redistributing their sock collections to make sure every sock was part of a pair. Phillip sat on a bench with a stack of paper and a set of markers, calling himself the Sock Drawer and offering to draw portraits of investors with their socks. Parents stood in the back, chatting and shrugging and saying things like "So *this* is a sock market" and "We didn't have anything like this in my day."

Fara thought it was all going along splendidly.

Tim shook Fara's hand. "Well done, Miss Ross," he said, bowing slightly. Sandra patted Fara on the back.

"Thank you, thank you," Fara said, only half jokingly. "I'm glad that everybody seems to be having a good time."

"Good?" said Tim. "Everybody's having a *great* time!"

Fara grinned. "I know," she admitted.

Suddenly the room became drenched in bright light. The sock market became loud and swollen with excitement. Fara turned to see two thick microphones on long sticks hovering overhead. A man entered the room, an enormous video camera on his shoulder. His jacket and the camera had matching yellow stickers with brown block lettering that clearly spelled "WSTV."

"WSTV!" said Zoë, patting Fara's shoulder repeatedly. "I can't believe I'm going to be on TV!"

A thin woman with yellow hair and a brown pantsuit stepped through the doorway and in front of the video camera. She quickly surveyed the room and then assumed a position directly in front of the INVEST IN THE SOCK MARKET sign. Phillip sat mesmerized on the bench to her left, a red marker making a deep dot on the paper where his hand had frozen mid-drawing. The woman cleared her throat and snapped on a smile. "This is Margaret Dengo for WSTV, reporting *live* from the first ever Stockville Sock Market," she announced for the camera.

All of the sock traders squealed, screeched, and fixed their hair. Mr. Ross nudged his wife and hissed, "Live, live! Go put in a videotape!" and she rushed into her husband's office to do just that. Teddy Ronkel turned on his own video camera to capture the process of broadcasting live television. Fara stayed close to the doorway behind a burly man holding one of the long microphones. *How did WSTV find out about this?* she asked herself. They couldn't have just seen Phillip's sign. She didn't know if the twitters in her stomach were due to thrill or dread. There was no way she could deny, even to herself, that this counted as outside publicity.

"I'm at Lane's Lanes bowling alley at a gathering organized by eleven-year-old *Fara Ross*," Margaret Dengo said as though Fara's name was one likely to be known at every gathering, "who is out to prove that what we wear on our feet every day is not to be taken for granted. In fact, she has helped all of those whose lives have been affected by *socks* to unite and face their concerns together. And from the excitement here at the Stockville Sock Market, it seems we might be at the start of a sock revolution." Margaret looked around and pointed at Tim, beckoning him to come forward and elaborate.

Tim pointed at himself, looked around, and moved toward Margaret with a walk so unnatural it seemed that he must be whispering to himself, "Left foot, right foot. Heel, then toe." But the moment the light hit his face, he came to life. "Fara is brilliant!" he said. "She helped me realize that I have the right to wear socks if I want to, and then she created this sock market so that we could all help each other. I bought these," he said, holding up the slip-resistant socks. "They're just what I needed."

Sandra stepped in next to him. "He bought them from my aunt!" she said, glowing with both nerves and pride. "When I read the article about Fara in the *Stockville Weekly Reporter*, I wrote to her to share my sock story. So I was so happy when she wrote me back a personal letter and invited me to a meeting. Because besides socks, everybody here just really cares about each other," she explained.

Tim nodded enthusiastically, visibly touched by Sandra's speech. "This is only our second meeting, but we've all made some awesome friends," he said. Then, as evidence, he put his arm around Sandra and gave the camera a thumbs-up.

The cameraman swiveled back to Margaret Dengo. "For those of you just tuning in," she said, "this is Margaret Dengo reporting live from Stockville's sock market, an idea conceived and implemented by Fara Ross, who is a sixth-grade student at Stockville Middle School. Let's see what exactly is taking place here at the market."

Lucy Gower leaped into the shot. "I'm going to trade socks with Fara," she said. "She's my friend."

Margaret Dengo bent down to one of Lucy's friends. "What's your name?" she asked.

The girl just looked at her, too nervous to talk.

"Do you like socks?" Margaret asked.

The girl nodded dumbly.

A boy in the corner shouted to turn the camera on him. "My name is Robert," he said, causing his circle of shoeless friends to snicker and say that his name was Robby. He ignored them and announced that his socks were unanimously the smelliest. Then he shouted, "I'm not going to vote for Melodee. I'm going to vote for Fara because then school won't sock! But school always socks," he added, and then fell over as though he'd made the joke of the century.

Fara slapped her forehead while the boys howled with laughter. This was not good. Not good.

Margaret Dengo smiled awkwardly and motioned for the camera to turn to Phillip. "Let's see what this young man is doing," she said.

Phillip's whole body was stiff. "I'm . . . um," he said, "drawing. Pictures. I'm the Sock Drawer." His father beamed.

Margaret smiled with her lips together. Tim jumped back

in front of the camera. "See," he said, "this sock market is a place to buy and sell and trade socks, but this whole thing is really about friendship. And being yourself. But Fara can explain it best."

"Yes!" said Margaret Dengo. "Let's see if we can get an appearance from the most noteworthy young woman in Stockville."

Fara tried to fade into the doorway, Mr. Z.'s words echoing in her mind. *Just manage to keep you and your socks out of the media for a few more days.* Why couldn't she seem to do that? How did WSTV find out about this? Anybody could have said something—Sandra, Tim, or someone else who didn't realize the consequences. She realized with a mix of hopelessness and reason that it didn't matter at this point anyway. Would it even save her if she managed to stay off the screen? It wasn't like she could deny that she was there; they were in her family's bowling alley. Everyone was proclaiming her name and actions on live television, and now the entire market was turned toward her, whispering her name and motioning for her to step in front of the camera.

Sandra rushed up to her and took her arm. "Come on," she whispered. "I was nervous too, but it's really not that bad. Margaret's nice."

"From the success of this event," Margaret Dengo

announced, "we might have to change our town's name to *Sockville*."

"C'mon, Fara," Tim called. "Give yourself some credit."

All right, Fara decided. *I will.*

Mrs. Ross had recorded the wrong channel, but it didn't matter because the segment aired again at 8:30, and at 10:00, and—according to Fara's uncle—at 1:15 a.m. By the time Fara crawled into bed with her journal on her lap, her parents had replayed it four times. "It's strange to see your own event on television," Fara wrote. She giggled, picturing the shot of Margaret Dengo, professional and composed, with Phillip's head, awkward and dazed, staring up at her from the bottom corner of the screen. *And yourself,* she thought, blushing and reflecting on her short interview. "First an article all about me in the newspaper," she wrote, "and then my first appearance on the news—and I'm not even twelve yet!" She blushed more thinking of what she heard her mother tell someone on the phone: "I know you have to be thirty-five to be president, but at this rate they might have to make an exception for her."

But she pushed the thought aside with a sharp shake of her freshly shampooed head. She had a more important presidency to concentrate on. One that she knew she would surely win, if only she was safe from punishment. It wouldn't really be fair for her to get in trouble for this, she reasoned. She hadn't invited WSTV; they had come on their own. They had just walked into her father's bowling alley without warning. "I'll just explain to Mr. Z. that Margaret Dengo and WSTV crashed the sock market," she wrote. "He'll understand."

With preposterous optimism she wondered if maybe she wouldn't have to explain at all. Using the rules of probability she'd been learning in math, she tried to calculate the odds that neither Mr. Z. nor Melodee had seen or heard about the news. Considering the speed with which information circulated in Stockville, the number of people from her school at the market, and the number of times it aired, she figured the odds were close to 1/1,000,000. "And that's not counting the way Melodee's mother seems to find out about everything," she wrote. She added a few zeros to her calculation, so that it now said "1/1,000,000,000."

"So," she said aloud before clicking off her light. "There's still a slight chance."

23. Sock Trauma

"FARA!" LUCY OPENED THE GOWERS' DOOR
right before Fara could knock. She wrapped her arms around
Fara's waist with such excitement that she drove her back,
causing them both to tumble off the porch and into the
grass. Fara heard the distinct crunch of her bagged lunch
from inside her backpack, which had taken the brunt of the
tackle. She hoped her books wouldn't be covered in vanilla
pudding. "That was so much fun last night," Lucy said as she
stood up and brushed herself off. "I was on the news," she
told Fara matter-of-factly.

"I saw," Fara responded. "You're famous."

Lucy grinned. "You're famouser," she said. "Jody wouldn't
even watch it," she continued. "We all watched it together—
our whole family, I mean. But Jody just sat in our room all
night scribbling in a notebook. On *my* top bunk, too. And

I told her to get off and she just ignored me. Mom said it's because she's becoming a teenager soon." Lucy shook her head. "Jody's so dumb."

"Thank you, Lucy," said Jody from the doorway. "Excuse me." She pushed her way through her sister and Fara and ran down the block.

Fara and Lucy looked at each other. Lucy shrugged. "Girls go through a lot of difficult changes at her age. We watched a video about it in school."

Fara tried not to laugh and rushed after Jody. Jody certainly *had* been acting like a teenager lately, running off without her and speaking only in short sentences. She missed the Jody who just last week in science had laughed so hard at the contents of a note from Fara that she had to grab the bathroom pass and sprint from the room. The one who'd plan out articles (for future publication, as she'd say) for each injustice Fara noticed in the world. She was thinking she might need that Jody later today, but it didn't look like her chances of having her were very good.

She quickly realized that her chances weren't very good at all. Jody wouldn't even look at her all morning. She turned in disgust when she passed her in the hallway. So did Vicki, with a sharp roll of her eyes, and so did Caroline, giving her a distinct look of disappointment before hiding her red face behind a book. Fara understood that they were probably upset about not being at the sock exchange. But she had had no idea that it would get so big. She needed to explain and apologize over lunch. But when she put down her squashed sandwich and dented pudding cup at their usual table, the conversation dried up.

"Who is this?" Vicki exclaimed with feigned shock. "Why in the world would *the* Fara Ross want to sit with us little people?" Caroline began to inspect her tuna fish, and Phillip dropped his cookie into his soup, but neither of them moved to stop Vicki. "She's too famous to invite us to her 'sock market,'" she continued, "yet she still eats lunch in the cafeteria like an ordinary sixth grader."

"I'm sorry," said Fara. "I was trying to keep everything small so I wouldn't attract any publicity."

Jody put down her string cheese and crossed her arms.

"Oh, yes," Vicki said as though someone had asked her to demonstrate sarcasm. "It looked like a very small gathering on television."

Even though she had prepared for this conversation, Fara's insides still felt as mushy as her lunch. "I didn't know that was going to happen."

"So I guess you figured it'd be safer to invite Melodee's campaign manager and the entire sixth grade over the people on your own campaign team, who used to consider themselves your friends."

Fara didn't know how to respond. Everything Vicki was saying was true, and all of the explanations she'd thought she'd use seemed silly now.

"Why don't you go sit with some high school people? Or some fourth graders, like Jody's sister? I'm sure anyone would be cooler than us."

The tables on either side of them were listening now. Melodee was especially absorbed; her tongue was running slowly over her pink braces, and her eyes were hungrily following the dialogue like she was watching a shark about to devour its prey in a nature special.

"I want to sit with you guys," Fara said quietly. She moved closer to Phillip. "Do you mind if I sit here, Phillip?"

Phillip inhaled loudly. "Um," he said. He looked from Fara to Vicki to Caroline to Jody and back.

"Go ahead," said Vicki. "Sit there. We'll leave. We don't want to take up chairs that you might need for all the people who want your autograph." She and Jody gathered their belongings and picked up their trays.

Caroline looked squarely at Fara before joining the other girls. "You could have at least told us about it before we saw it on TV," she said.

Fara felt her face get hot.

"Are you coming, Phillip?" Vicki asked.

Phillip looked physically torn. Fara sighed. "Don't bother," she said. "Don't make him choose. I'll go sit somewhere else."

"Oh," said Vicki in her best newscaster voice. "What a good person. What a great role model for sixth graders everywhere."

Fara's chest started to burn.

"Yeah," said Jody. "Way to make a statement, Fars."

Fara stared at her for a moment and then turned around. Of course her best friend knew exactly what would hurt the most. She concentrated on the exit and tried to appear composed as she made her way to it. *Please, please, please don't cry until you're out of the cafeteria,* she prayed. *Please.* Fara walked right past Mean Jean, ignoring her questions and warnings. Her tears threatened to spill over the moment she reached the hallway, but she resolved to keep them in thirty seconds longer so she could make it to the second-floor bathroom, where there were likely to be fewer people. She didn't need groups of girls fussing over her and asking if she was all right, then circulating an exaggerated report of what had happened. She took the stairs two at a time and turned so sharply on the landing that she literally crashed into someone. She looked up. Mr. Z.

"Fara," Mr. Z. said in surprise. And then he said it again,

this time more hesitantly and with a slight frown. "Do you have a minute?" he asked, checking his watch.

Fara nodded glumly. What else could possibly have come next? She followed him down the hall and into his empty classroom. Mr. Z. leaned against the front of his desk. "Have a seat," he said. "Fara, I'll cut right to the chase. I watched WSTV last night."

"I didn't have anything to do with it," Fara tried. "Honest. They just showed up."

Mr. Z. sighed and smoothed his hair. "I assume you're talking about the TV station and not the sock traders." She nodded, too scared to do anything else. "You may not have had anything to do with the television crew coming," he continued, "but you did have everything to do with the sock market. You wrote personal letters to people and invited them to two meetings. You must have known that you might be inviting publicity. And even if no media had come, you had half the school there. You can't say you didn't know that that would affect the course of the election."

"But, Mr. Z.—"

"There have been complaints, and rightly so," he said with a shrug of disappointment. "We promised all of the candidates that this would be a friendly and fair election."

"But I wasn't doing anything wrong," she argued, trying to convince not only him, but all of her friends and herself.

Why doesn't anybody understand that? she thought.

"No," he agreed. "But admirable as your intentions may have been, you were still taking a risk doing this so close to the voting." He sighed and stood up. "I have to be fair. I have students and parents counting on me for that. You broke the rules, Fara. You are disqualified from the election."

Fara inhaled sharply. "But," she said, "I really want this. It's not just for the popularity or something. I have really good ideas, and . . . and . . ."

"I know, Fara," he said, crossing his arms. "That's why this whole thing is so disappointing."

Fara sniffed. As she rose, all of her emotions rushed down. She should be proud of herself for making such an impact, like she was last night. But she wasn't allowed to feel that. Instead she felt a swirl of anger, guilt, and dread, which only intensified when she realized she had no friends to make it go away. A slow panic crept through her system. Sock trauma.

The bell rang to signal the end of lunch. Fara took her backpack and headed numbly through the hallway and down the stairs to the nurse's office. "I feel sick," she announced in the doorway. "I need to go home."

Fara didn't talk to her father on the ride back to their house, nor did she talk to her mother when she got home from work. She sat on her bed, legs crossed, journal out, tear splotches on the one sentence she'd written over and over again, like it was a punishment: "I got disqualified." At 5:30 her mother knocked gently on her door and asked if she wanted any dinner. Fara slid a note through the opening at the bottom of the door: "No." The last time she'd done that she was six years old and had been sent to her room for using a bad word. She thought she heard her mother giggling as she picked it up, but she didn't care. She heard her parents laughing in the kitchen, and then another note came back a minute later: "Do you want to talk about it? Circle one: Yes. No. Maybe later." She hoped her mother could feel her cold stare through the door. "No," she shot back.

She stayed in her room the whole evening, emerging only to go to the bathroom and to make herself a bowl of granola with milk after she was sure her father had left for Lane's Lanes and her mother was in her room for the night. It felt good to sit in the dark kitchen with the television on so low she could barely hear it; she was away from all of her taunting sock paraphernalia. Just when things were starting to look up—just when she was starting to forget how much she hated socks, and just when she was *this* close to winning the presidency and moving past her socky image once and for all—socks had ruined her life once again. *I hate socks more than ever,* she thought as she heard her father's car pull up and she put her bowl in the dishwasher. Then, as she clicked off the television, she knew exactly what she needed. Tomorrow she would call an emergency meeting of the Sockinental Congress.

24. A Dismal, Socky Future

"PLEASE, HONEY, I'M GLAD TO SEE YOU OUT of your room, but stop that tapping. I'm trying to do work here."

Fara flattened her hand on the dining-room table, where she was sitting opposite her mother and three stacks of paper. She didn't realize she'd been tapping. Sandra and Tim were ten minutes late. But at least they were coming. Tim had said that he was busy, but he didn't mention that his plans were to hang out with Sandra; Fara found that out only when Sandra said that she and Tim could both stop by for a few minutes on their way to an afternoon movie.

Fara caught her fingers midtap and apologized to her mother. Eleven minutes late. She had called Zoë, but her dad had said she was out, without offering further explanation, and she didn't have the guts to call Phillip. She needed people who hated socks to listen to her and say they understood.

Twelve minutes late. She needed Sandra and Tim to show up.

The doorbell rang. Fara leaped up and answered it. "Come on in," she said, not caring that she sounded far too excited to see them.

But Sandra shook her pudgy head. "We can't really stay long," she said. "Our movie starts in twenty minutes, and Tim's sister is driving." She pointed to an old, boxy car sputtering in Fara's driveway with a finicky-looking teenage girl mouthing radio lyrics behind the wheel. "But I'm glad you called," Sandra said. "I really wanted to thank you for helping me. After the WSTV thing a lot of people have been talking to me about my aunt's socks and stuff. I've never been so popular," she said with a faint blush.

"That's great," Fara said. She looked down at Tim's feet. "You're wearing socks!" she said to him.

"Yup," said Tim. "My grandpa liked the ones Sandra's aunt made me. And we got to talking, and I made him understand that socks can be safe. So I wanted to thank you too."

"No problem," Fara said quickly. She wanted to tell them the story of her day yesterday, but before she could begin, Tim's sister beeped the car horn.

"Well, it was really good to see you," said Sandra. "The sock exchange was a lot of fun."

"Yeah," Fara said. "I need your help with something, but I guess it can wait until Thursday's meeting."

Sandra and Tim looked at each other. "Well," Tim said, "I don't think I'm going to be at the meeting."

Fara wrinkled her forehead, hoping they'd think she was squinting in the sun.

"I mean," he continued, "I'm all set now. I don't really need a sock support group."

Fara looked at Sandra.

"Yeah," she said. "I don't think I'm going to go this week either. Maybe in the future, though," she added hopefully. But she might as well have not even said it; Fara knew it wasn't true.

Tim's sister honked again.

"You're a cool kid," Tim said, ruffling her hair as though she were five, or a puppy. "Good luck with the election and everything. But you probably don't need it."

"Yeah," added Sandra. "Hey, as of Monday you can start being known for something other than socks!"

Fara started to nod, but what did it matter if she played along? Clearly, her contribution to the world would never go above the feet.

Tim's sister leaned her elbow into the horn.

"We'd really better go," Tim said. "But thanks for everything, Fara," he called as he walked down the steps. "Especially for letting me meet Sandra!"

Sandra giggled and jokingly punched him in the shoulder. Then he lightly pushed her into the car and climbed into the backseat next to her. Fara watched the car pull sloppily out of the driveway. All of her excitement, her hope, her fitful night's sleep and her finger tapping, left her alone on her stoop with one dull yellow sock, one pale purple sock, and another round of disappointment. She wanted to help people, right? She wanted to make a difference. Yet she was too selfish to be happy for Sandra and Tim, and that made her feel even crummier.

She dragged herself back inside and called some members of the Sockinental Congress to tell them that Thursday's meeting was canceled. After a few of them failed to sound disappointed or said that they hadn't been planning on attending anyway, she gave up and slumped into a chair in the living room. "Far," her mother called. "Dad and I decided to run a clothing drive at the bowling alley starting next month. So go through your closet and your sock drawers and put anything you don't want in a bag. Maybe that Red Sox shirt? Or that tie Uncle Barry gave you."

Fara looked down at her mismatched socks, which together made up the colors of a bruise. As much as she'd been looking forward to stripping off her socks and starting fresh, she wanted to start fresh from *somewhere*. She wanted to exchange "Fara Ross, Sock Girl" for "Fara Ross, Class President"—not for "Fara Ross, Unoriginal, Friendless Loser." At this rate she would never be able to give any of her sock items away. And even if she did, they'd only get replenished on her next birthday. "It doesn't matter, Mom," she said.

Her mother sighed. The doorbell rang. Zoë. Fara once again stood out on her stoop with someone whose impatient older sibling was in a car in the driveway. "I just stopped by to see how you were doing," Zoë said. "Socks about the election."

Fara managed a small giggle.

"I only helped Melodee because her mom always ordered good food for our team meetings. I didn't actually want her to win."

Fara told her about Sandra and Tim.

"That's awesome that the Sockinental Congress helped them," said Zoë, cracking her gum. She looked down at Fara's feet. "Hey, why are you still doing the sock thing?" A honk of the horn covered Fara's sigh. "Well, I guess I'll see you around," Zoë said before walking toward the car. "But seriously, you should just stop mismatching if you don't want to do it anymore."

Fara went inside. Nobody understood anything. Her stupid socks were the only worthwhile thing about her now. The thing that made her known for doing something good, so that she'd be able to do something bigger. But she'd gotten disqualified from the something bigger she had been planning for since June, and now the something bigger that had happened by mistake was falling apart as quickly and unintentionally as it had come together. She felt like she'd been transported back in time to the day of elementary school graduation, when Melodee stole the Harvey Award and left her and her signature socks to look for a new way to become known for making a difference. And how could she do anything if she was known for nothing?

As Fara sank back into the chair in the living room, she pictured herself in eighty years as a bitter celebrity at the nursing home—a wrinkly, hunched woman with mismatched socks sticking out of her orthopedic shoes.

25. Terror, Horror, Doom

EVEN IF FARA HAD NEVER INTENDED TO RUN for student council, she would have been eager to have one less class on election day. But there was nothing to look forward to on Monday. Her mother refused to let her stay home, claiming that successfully moping through the entire weekend was enough, so Fara had no choice but to parade down to the assembly with the rest of the school during eighth period. Since there was no use sneaking away from her class to be near Jody or Phillip, she sat sandwiched between the only two other people who stuck with the teacher, both of whom Fara was sure rarely showered.

Even though Melodee was running unopposed, she still gave a speech, and it was filled with promises of suggestion boxes, school spirit, and a fun year. Melodee caught Fara's eye when she started proclaiming how proud and honored she was to be student council president, and how Stockville Middle School could be sure that she was the best person for the job. "Last year I won the Harvey Award for an Outstanding Graduate, so you know that I will be a good president. This is where I would say 'Best of luck' to the other candidate and tell you to vote for me," Melodee concluded, "but I don't have to because I've already won. So instead I will say that you will not be disappointed—the words 'president' and 'Melodee' are a perfect *match*. Thank you." It made Fara want to puke.

A cold thunderstorm began to move through Stockville late Monday night, and the darkness of her room on Tuesday morning only compounded Fara's lack of desire to get out of bed and spend seven hours in a place where the leader of the student body was Melodee Simon. While Fara lethargically pushed around oatmeal with her spoon, her father asked if he needed to pick up Jody on the way to school. "What's going on between you two?" he asked. Fara just shrugged and left the table.

The election results were announced during homeroom, and Melodee sat gloating and proud, as though she'd been elected Miss America. She nodded in approval at Tania Farucci winning secretary and Kyle Degala winning treasurer. When soccer-player-Neil was announced vice president,

Melodee turned to the girl behind her and whispered "Yes!" then turned to Fara and winked. Fara rolled her eyes and looked away. If Melodee honestly thought that being student council president was going to make her popular like the other officers—or make her soccer-player-Neil's girlfriend!—she was in for a terrible awakening. *Student council usually does nothing,* Fara thought angrily. *But now all the other officers will hate working with the president so much that they will do* extra *nothing.*

Phillip's glance of sympathy and various people's comments through the hallway that Fara should have won made things slightly better, but she still sulked through the day feeling as dreary as her thick, wet, gray and brown socks. She missed Jody even more than she had when the Gowers spent two weeks visiting family in the Midwest last summer. "Strange how you can miss someone when you're in the same place," she wrote in her journal that night. She wondered if Jody or her other friends missed her. It didn't seem like it from the way they chatted and laughed during lunch on Tuesday and Wednesday. Only Phillip even seemed to notice her at a quiet table toward the front of the cafeteria. He gave her a small wave on Wednesday, but Fara saw him shake his head when he turned back to the others, probably denying that he'd waved to anyone.

By the time Fara decided to look through the *Stockville*

Weekly Reporter on Wednesday afternoon, she didn't know how much more she could take of feeling glum. After skimming the one letter to the editor about how fun the sock exchange had been, she flipped past the page-two article announcing the new middle school student council officers, complete with a photograph in which Melodee stood between Mr. Z. and soccer-player-Neil, her braces reflecting in the flash. On page four, however, she caught something that captured her full attention.

WHEN FRIENDSHIP ISN'T FRIENDSHIP

An Editorial

by Young Journalist Jody Gower

Being in middle school can be very tough. Teachers pour on homework, multiple tests occur on the same day, and what someone else thinks of you can make you popular or leave you alone at lunch. What usually helps middle school students is having a best friend or best group of friends to get them through it. I always thought that best friends are supposed to stay by your side and not mind sharing or even giving up the spotlight sometimes. Sometimes it is hard to be that best friend because you feel like you are always in second place, but you know that the other person will be there for you. But I recently learned that even a so-called best friend can desert you and replace you without thinking twice.

Parents say that friends come and go and the true ones will stick by you in the end. That might be true, and I hope that it will be for me.

But here's some advice to everyone in middle school: If you want to do good things for people, don't forget about the people closest to you in the process.

Fara closed the newspaper. Her glumometer had reached its limit. It was time to take action.

26. Sock Therapy

"FARA!" MRS. GOWER CRIED. SHE PULLED HER
inside and wrapped her in a tight embrace. "It's so good to
see you."

Stepping inside the Gowers' house made Fara feel the
way she had when she came across her old stuffed monkey
in a box in the attic—like she had recovered a part of herself. Dean woofed and panted at her feet while she laid her
jacket on the jacket chair. It was nice to see that some things
hadn't changed since she'd been here last. After Fara had
convinced Mrs. Gower that she and her parents were doing
well, Mrs. Gower let her go up to Jody's room.

"Hi," Fara said with a quiet tap on the door. Jody looked
up from her desk.

A twiglike body with a mass of curly hair suddenly flew
from the top bunk and landed inches from Fara. "Hello!"

Lucy said. "Thanks for coming to hang out with me."

Fara hugged Lucy back but then stepped away. "Actually," she said, "I came to talk to Jody. So do you think we can hang out here for a little while . . . alone?"

"Boo," Lucy said with a pout. "Fine." She stuck her tongue out at Jody and shut the door loudly behind her. But then, probably for fear of losing Fara's friendship completely, she shouted, "Sorry!" before scampering downstairs.

Jody turned around in her desk chair. "Thank you," she whispered.

"I have a major problem and I need to erupt," Fara said, hoping Jody would at least listen to the three sentences she'd been practicing the whole run there. "Socks have ruined my life again. They made me lose my best friend."

Jody didn't say anything for a few long seconds. Fara didn't say anything either. But she did ease herself down onto Jody's bottom bunk, and Jody didn't object. *Okay so far,* Fara thought. When Jody didn't say anything for another few seconds, Fara continued. "I'm sorry, Jode. I got carried away. But I didn't mean to hurt you. Honest." Fara could tell that Jody wasn't convinced. "I've missed you so much," she continued. "The past few days have socked—I mean, they were terrible. I'm sorry. I won't bring up socks ever again if you don't want me to."

Jody gave a half smile. "Really?"

"Absolutely."

"That might be difficult."

"I don't care. I'll do whatever it takes."

Jody tapped her pen against her lips. She jumped up and sprinted from the room. She returned a moment later with a pair of gym socks from the hamper. "My dad was telling me about something he does to help people stop smoking. But let's see . . ."

Fara wasn't sure where this was going, but at least Jody was talking. She didn't ask questions, just moved over so Jody could sit opposite her on the bed.

"Now," Jody said. "Close your eyes and think about trying to save the world from sock problems. And take a deep breath in through your nose."

Fara played along. She thought. She breathed. "Ew, gross!" she said. She opened her eyes and found Jody holding the sweaty gym socks right up to her nose.

Jody laughed. "Think about the past week or so that you spent without me," she said. Then she pushed the rancid socks even closer to Fara's nostrils.

Fara wrinkled her nose and turned her head. "I get it! I get it!"

Jody followed Fara's nose with the socks. "Keep thinking! Keep smelling!" she said through laughter. Fara squirmed and squealed, but Jody wouldn't let her get away. "Think about being famous, and keep breeeathing deeeply!" she sang.

Fara covered her face with her hands. "Enough!" she cried with enough drama to win a Daytime Emmy. "I'll never do it again! This is torture! Please, Jode, stop!"

Jody collapsed in a fit of laughter. "Now whenever you think of trying to help people with socks, you'll think of that smell and come hang out with me instead."

Fara took exaggeratedly deep breaths to recover. "That was disgusting. Smell your hands," she dared Jody.

"Gross! No way!"

Fara moved to force Jody's fingers to her nose, but Jody screeched and climbed the ladder up to the top bunk. Fara banged on the bed from below but then gave up and lay down. When their laughter died down, they tried to catch their breath. "Heeee," breathed Jody.

"Heeeee," breathed Fara, louder and breathier.

"Heee-eee-eee," Jody breathed back.

"Hooooo!" said Fara.

"Hoo-oooo hooo!" said Jody.

"Woof!" said Dean, who had crawled in to join the fun.

Both girls broke down again. When they were finally calm, Fara held up her arm. "Here," she said. "You'll probably need that."

Jody flopped onto her stomach and reached down to pull the hair tie off Fara's wrist. "Thanks," she said. She sighed. "I don't mind if you keep wearing your socks to show that you don't think Melodee is a good *match* for president. Can you believe she said that?"

Fara made a gagging noise and shifted in the bunk so that her camouflage and polka-dotted feet stuck out into the room. "Are you sure?"

"Yeah. I mean," Jody continued, "I know you're the one who's going to run for president and I'm only the one who's going to write articles about you. But if my articles help you become president, then you could at least say thank you or something."

"I know. I think I'll make you chief of staff. Or head speechwriter. No—both! Or secretary of state. Or—"

"That's enough."

Fara smiled. "And no matter which position you want, you will have your own room in the White House. With a top bunk."

Jody grinned. "Thanks," she said.

"Of course, that's only if I become president. I'll probably be stuck as the spokesperson for a sock company or something."

From their parallel beds they discussed her disqualification. "If you really didn't invite WSTV, who did?" Jody asked.

"It could have been anyone."

Jody sat up. "Do you think someone might have done it on purpose?"

Fara shrugged. The thought had crossed her mind.

"Well then, let's do some research," Jody said. "My next article could be a piece of investigative journalism!"

Fara didn't really want her name in the newspaper again, but she was so happy to have Jody back on her side that she didn't complain. Jody climbed down and gathered her reporting gear. But before they left to start their interviews, she said that she needed to make sure that the sock therapy would stick. She took a freshly washed pair of socks from the pile of clean laundry on her dresser. Holding them to Fara's nose, she chanted in a spooky, low voice, "Think about Jody, think about Jody. . . ."

Fara smiled and breathed in the refreshing aroma. "Mm!" she said. "I will never forget."

27. The Sock-ic Is In

THE SIGHT OF FARA AND JODY TOGETHER ON his porch made Phillip close the screen door on his toes. "You guys are—you're—everything's—?" he asked while hopping about.

"Yes," Jody said. "Are you okay?"

Phillip shook his head. The girls followed him inside and sat him down in the family room. Fara went to the kitchen, took a bag of frozen lima beans out of the freezer, and placed it on Phillip's foot before sitting on the floor next to the coffee table. While he recovered, Fara looked at the piles of interesting books and magazines that were stacked about the room. Her own house was spick-and-span, Jody's was lived-in and worn, and Phillip's was somewhere in between. Large photographs of the family adorned the walls, but they were all slightly off center or uneven, as Phillip's dad was very much like Phillip. Fara noticed a new addition to one wall, however: one of her campaign posters that Phillip had drawn. She pointed to it.

Phillip shrugged sheepishly. "My dad likes that one. I'm saving them for my portfolio," he explained. "Unless you want them back, of course."

Fara said she didn't mind.

"You know I said I wasn't okay before because of my foot and not because you guys are friends again," Phillip said.

The girls laughed. "We know," said Jody.

"Because I'm really glad you guys are friends again. It was terrible when you weren't."

"We know," Jody repeated.

"I didn't mean to ignore you all week," Phillip continued to Fara. "But I didn't know who to choose."

"I know," Fara said. "Let's not talk about it anymore."

Phillip moved the lima beans to the coffee table. "I can't believe Melodee is president!" he said with sudden vehemence. "Oh," he said quickly. "Should we not talk about that, either?"

Jody laughed. "No, it's okay to talk about that."

"Okay," said Phillip. "That's so unfair! Nobody wants Melodee to be president. Not Caroline, not Vicki—even though she might say she does, I know she doesn't—not even Jamie Orsino or that group. I heard them talking in math."

"Thanks," said Fara.

"Do you have any idea who could have told WSTV about the sock market?" Jody asked. Phillip opened his mouth. "Wait!" Jody said. She took out her memo pad and pen. "Okay, go."

"I have no idea."

Jody wrote that down. "We're trying to figure it out."

"We should go ask Margaret Dengo," Phillip said.

"I don't think she'd know," Fara said. "I think someone else just tells her where to go and why."

Phillip looked disappointed. "Oh, right," he said.

"Could it have been Zoë?" Jody asked.

Fara shook her head. "I don't think so. She seemed really excited and surprised when they showed up."

"Yeah, but she was the head of Melodee's campaign. And she knew that if you had more publicity, something would happen, because she was at the meeting."

"I know," said Fara, trying to tread cautiously. She didn't want to defend Zoë so much that Jody thought she liked Zoë more than her. She noticed that Phillip was keeping quiet. "Maybe. But she didn't even want Melodee to win. She was only helping her because her mom always ordered good food for their meetings."

Jody looked up from her memo pad, where she had been furiously transcribing the entire conversation. "Just for good food? Don't you think that's a little suspicious? I think she's hiding something."

"I don't know, Jode. At that first meeting it didn't seem like she and Melodee liked each other at all, remember?"

"Maybe it's all part of an act. They're secretly best friends!"

"Zoë and Melodee?" asked Phillip, eyebrows raised.

"Melodee! I bet she did it," Jody said suddenly. "But how did she find out? This will make a great story. Front-page stuff."

"Cool," said Phillip. "We could ask people at the sock meeting tomorrow."

Fara told Phillip the meeting was canceled. She wrinkled her nose. "Even the thought of the Sockinental Congress makes me sick!" she told Jody.

Jody laughed. "Yum, sweaty gym socks."

Phillip laughed even though he didn't get the joke. They filled him in on sock therapy. "That's so cool," he said. "Does your dad really do that as a psychologist?"

"Yes," Jody said. Then she broke down laughing. "So that means I'm a sock-ologist," she managed to blurt out.

"So can you read people's minds and see who told WSTV about the sock exchange?" Phillip asked, his eyes wide.

Fara grinned. "She's a sock-ologist, not a sock-ic!"

"I don't get it," said Phillip. "Why is she a socket?"

Jody rolled off the couch, holding her stomach.

"No! Sock-*ic*!" Fara said. "Like 'psychic.'"

"Oh," said Phillip. "I get it! I think."

Jody got up and ran to the bathroom.

While Phillip tried to explain why it wouldn't make sense for Jody to be a socket in the wall, Fara just sat back and grinned. It didn't matter who had told WSTV or why. Melodee was already president, and there was nothing she could do about it. If Jody or Phillip were sock-ic, she thought, they'd know that she was simply enjoying every minute with them, and she wouldn't trade that away for any presidency.

28. The President's Mistake

"DO YOU LIKE MY SKIRT, TANIA?" MELODEE
asked.

"Sure, whatever."

"It was *really* expensive, but I just fell in love with it."

Tania let go of the piece of her hair that she was examining. "Can we just start the meeting? I have to get to track."

The two boys nodded and chewed on the doughnuts from Loretta's Bake Stop that Melodee's mother had dropped off. The four officers were gathered in Mr. Z.'s room, but Mr. Z. was in the teachers' lounge photocopying handouts for the next day. Melodee was sitting on his desk. "Okay, well, first of all, I just wanted to say that I hope that you guys think of me as not only your leader, but your friend."

Kyle looked at Neil and mouthed, "Yeah, right." Tania saw it and started to giggle.

"What's funny?" Melodee asked.

"Nothing," said Tania. "Go on."

Melodee crossed her arms. "Tell me," she ordered.

"It was nothing," Neil said. "We're just enjoying our doughnuts."

"Good. My mom can bring food to every meeting. She wants us to work closely with the PTA. But that shouldn't be too hard, since she's the president of the PTA and I'm the president of us."

In the margin of her secretary notebook Tania drew a figure that resembled Melodee and put a speech bubble that said, "Blah blah blah! Me me me!" She slid it to Kyle and he snickered loudly.

"What?" demanded Melodee.

"Nothing," said Tania as she added a big, ugly skirt to the figure. Kyle laughed harder.

"Tell me," said Melodee.

Tania drew steam coming out of the figure's ears. Kyle laughed louder. Melodee got up and Tania covered the drawing with her hand.

"Move your hand," said Melodee.

"I can rest my hand wherever I want," said Tania.

"Move it."

"You're student council president, not hand-resting-place president."

Kyle let out a loud laugh. He moved his hand onto Neil's doughnut.

"Move your hand," said Tania to Kyle. "You'll upset the hand-resting-place president!"

"Fine," said Melodee. "Forget it. This meeting is canceled."

"Oh, come on," said Neil.

"No," said Melodee. "I don't know what you're laughing at, but I'm not going to put up with it."

"Fine with me," said Tania. She closed her notebook.

Kyle put on his backpack. He reached for another doughnut, but Melodee pulled the box away. Kyle stared at her in disbelief. "Now you won't let me have a doughnut?" he said. "It's not my fault you couldn't handle our first meeting."

Melodee stared him down.

Kyle shook his head. "No one would have even voted for her," he said to Tania as they left. "She just got lucky."

"It doesn't matter!" Melodee called after them.

Soccer-player-Neil sighed and stood up.

"You can tell them I didn't just get lucky," Melodee said to him while he put on his jacket. "Fara deserved to get caught, and I deserved to win."

"Whatever," said Neil. "You know you really didn't *do* any-thing to win."

Melodee scoffed. "Didn't do anything? You don't think WSTV just *happened* to show up at the sock market, do you?"

Mr. Z. appeared in the doorway, his hands full of photo-copied maps and worksheets. "What was that, Melodee?"

29. Principal Cluver

ANYONE WHO PASSED FARA AND JODY ON Thursday morning would have guessed they were in a flowery meadow on a warm spring day instead of on the sidewalks that led to Stockville Middle School on the coldest day of the year so far. They chatted and laughed and caught up on all the funny things that had happened during the week that they didn't speak. Jody told Fara how milk had come out of her nose after her brother farted at dinner, causing them both to be sent to their rooms. "But it was so worth it," Jody said. Fara told Jody how Mike Dulaney had asked to go to the bathroom during Spanish and came back twenty minutes later with an ice cream sandwich. "So then he had to stand in front of the class and describe the entire process of buying the ice cream sandwich in Spanish," Fara said.

Seeing that Melodee's seat was empty in homeroom made

Fara's day even brighter than she could have asked for. "Maybe her perfume was so smelly that stray dogs started chasing after her on her way to school," Fara mused to Phillip.

"I'm pretty sure Melodee wouldn't walk to school," Phillip said.

Fara laughed. Then Phillip laughed a moment later when he realized that what he'd said was funny. "Or maybe she's at the orthodontist because she talked so much her braces broke," he tried.

"Or because she has such a big mouth that the orthodontist has to schedule special, extra-long appointments for her," Fara said.

A few people near them overheard and joined in the game, but all of the laughter stopped when the intercom buzzed and the principal's voice instructed their homeroom teacher to send Fara Ross to his office immediately. Everyone oohed.

Fara looked at Phillip. What could this be about?

Phillip gave a hopeful gasp. "Maybe the principal realized Mr. Z. made a mistake, and he wants to apologize and make you president."

"I don't know about that," said Fara. Although it had crossed her mind. But she doubted it. On the other hand, she was pretty sure she had to be done being in trouble by now.

"I don't think you could be in trouble again," said Phillip. But his tone of voice revealed that he wasn't quite sure.

"You read my mind," Fara said.

Phillip grinned. "I'm sock-ic!" he said.

While Phillip made sure the people around him understood the pun, Fara took the hall pass her teacher had written and headed out. She took the long way to the principal's office so that she could walk by Jody's homeroom and see if she had any clue as to what this could be about (or at the very least communicate in mysterious hand and facial signals from the doorway), but Jody was intently staring out the window with her pen pressed to her lips, and Fara had no way of getting her attention and not the teacher's.

From the shaking of her legs on her way downstairs she realized that she was nervous. The last time she'd been called down to the principal's office, she was in third grade and had won the Help Stockville Stay Stunning essay contest. She replayed the past week in her head, trying to think of something she'd done that could have gotten her in trouble.

The secretary was on the phone when Fara entered the office, so she took a step back and waited. She realized her hands were shaking. She wished she could just get this over with. "Yo," came a gruff voice from behind her. She turned to see a boy slouched in a chair against the wall. She and Jody often passed him and his friends hanging out by the back gates on their way home from school. She didn't know his name, but it was rumored that he had his own parole officer. It was also rumored that it had taken him three years to pass the sixth grade. Fara wasn't sure if that was true, but it would help explain his almost-full mustache. "Yo," he said again. "You're that sock girl, right?"

Fara's mouth dropped open. She quickly closed it and tried to act cool. "Um . . . yeah," she said. "Yeah."

"So your socks are all crazy today?" he asked.

"Yeah," she said again.

He motioned with his chin. "Show me," he said.

Fara lifted the legs of her corduroys to show him a striped sock and a neon green sock.

"That's messed up," the boy said.

Tell me about it, Fara thought.

The secretary hung up the phone and apologized. Then she buzzed the principal and told Fara to go right in, they were waiting for her. She gulped.

When Fara opened the door, she was not entirely surprised to be greeted by Melodee's folded arms and usual *What's that vile smell?* face. She was completely surprised, however, to find Mr. Z., Zoë, soccer-player-Neil, and Melodee's mother in addition to Mr. Cluver, whom she recognized as the principal only from the "Welcome, New

Middle Schoolers!" morning a few months ago.

Mr. Z. was wearing his usual Beatles tie but was dressed formally in black pants instead of khaki cargos. His hair was gelled back and neatly tied. Fara guessed that he must have known he'd be meeting with the principal and Ms. Simon. Yet despite all of this, he looked ragged and worn out, like he had had to fix a flat tire on his bicycle before coming to work. "Good morning, Fara," he said.

"Have a seat, please," added Mr. Cluver.

She did.

"In fact," he said, "why don't you all have a seat?"

They all did, with the exception of Ms. Linda Simon. When Melodee saw that her mother had remained standing, she stood up again.

"Is this everyone involved?" the principal asked.

"I believe so," said Mr. Z.

"I'm not involved," said Zoë.

"We haven't started discussing anything yet," said Mr. Z. in a distinct tone of warning and with a glance toward the principal.

Mr. Cluver asked Zoë to please be patient and Mr. Z. to please describe why they were all called together like this. Mr. Z. began by talking about Jody's first article, and Melodee and Ms. Simon's response. He then recounted their first meeting, in which he distinctly told both candidates that they were not allowed to have any more outside publicity.

"Is this correct?" Mr. Cluver asked. "Both of you knew that there was to be no more outside publicity?"

Fara nodded along with Melodee. She wished they would cut to the stuff she didn't already know. Why was Melodee's mother there? And how could Neil possibly be involved? Her mind was overflowing with possibilities. Her favorite was that Neil had protested serving under Melodee and insisted on starving himself until Fara be made student council president instead. But among the many reasons that that was implausible, she knew that it wouldn't really require a group meeting with Mr. Cluver. And an empty Kudos bar wrapper was sticking out of Neil's pocket.

"Is that correct, Fara?" the principal asked. "That Mr. Zolitski disqualified you from the election because of the segment about your sock exchange on WSTV?"

"Yes," said Fara. She started paying attention again. Unless Mr. Z. somehow knew that she had lost her friends and that the Sockinental Congress had failed and that she had sulked around her house for days, she figured the new information was about to surface.

"So Melodee ran unopposed and won the presidency," Mr. Z. said. "And she held the first student council meeting yesterday afternoon. When I got to the meeting—I was a little bit late—they had adjourned except for Melodee and

Neil, and Melodee was saying that the television station didn't just *happen* to show up at the sock exchange."

"That's right!" said Neil before Mr. Cluver could ask.

Melodee humphed. "But, Mr. Cluver—"

"Wait a moment," he answered. "Unless you'd like to finish the story for Mr. Zolitski."

Melodee turned to her mother, who looked at her sternly over her pursed lips.

Fara was on the edge of her seat. Jody had been right to question how WSTV had heard about the market after all! She was going to be disappointed that she hadn't uncovered this story herself. Maybe Mr. Cluver would agree to be interviewed.

"So," continued Mr. Z., untying and retying his ponytail, "after some time Melodee confessed that her mother had played a role in helping WSTV learn about the sock market. Of course I was amazed to hear this—you don't expect this sort of thing from middle school politics!—so I arranged this meeting to sort everything out with all of the people involved."

Zoë let out a low whistle. "Woah!" she said.

"I take it you didn't know about this until now, then?" asked Mr. Cluver.

"No way!" said Zoë. "I told you I wasn't involved. I had no clue it would be this dirty. Geez, Melodee."

"Frank," said Ms. Simon.

"Call me Mr. Cluver," the principal said coldly.

Ms. Simon raised her eyebrows. "Mr. Cluver, then," she said. "My daughter was very upset when this Ross girl was the subject of an entire article in the town newspaper. She was the better candidate for the position and she knew it, but you know how these elections are. An article can make someone popular, and that could make the other students overlook valid qualifications."

Mr. Cluver asked how Ms. Simon had found out about the market, and she stuck her nose in the air and said Philbert's father had casually mentioned it to her at a PTA meeting. "That's not *my* fault," she said with a chuckle.

Fara was fuming, but she was too polite to argue with a parent in front of the principal.

Luckily, Zoë wasn't. "That doesn't mean you go and get the other candidate disqualified! Geez, Aunt Linda!"

Aunt Linda! Fara thought. Zoë had been hiding something after all!

Neil's big gray eyes met Fara's; he couldn't believe it either. Zoë shot them both a look that said, *Isn't it terrible that we're related? Please, please don't tell.*

"I am an adult," said Ms. Simon calmly, "and *you*"—she gave Zoë a look that showed she wasn't proud of their connection either—"will treat me with respect."

Zoë let out a laugh.

"At any rate, Frank—I mean, *Mr. Cluver*—I take *complete* responsibility for this little fiasco. But clearly you cannot remove my daughter from a position she has already won because *I* made a mistake."

"Exactly," said Melodee, who had been itching to get a word in. "I didn't really do anything."

Neil started to laugh quietly.

"What?" fired Melodee.

"Well, I told you you didn't really do anything to win," he said.

Fara and Zoë giggled.

Mr. Cluver stood up. "So neither of you had anything to do with this besides what was already mentioned?" he asked Zoë and Neil. They shook their heads. "You may return to class, then," he said. "And I know you probably will anyway, but please try not to say anything about this to the other students until it is completely resolved."

They all could hear Zoë and Neil excitedly chattering once they left the room, so it was clear that Mr. Cluver's request didn't stand a chance.

"Mr. Cluver," said Ms. Simon gently. "I would like to figure a way out of this that doesn't involve the PTA or the superintendent or the school board. I'm *sure* you want the full support of the PTA and the community, especially with the budget vote coming up. Let's work something out," she said. "But please, don't punish Melodee for something that doesn't concern her. She will make an excellent student council president."

"Ms. Simon!" said Mr. Z. abruptly. "There is no way Melodee can remain student council president."

"Zach—"

"Call me Mr. Zolitski."

"Mr. Zolitski, there is no way that Fara Ross can be appointed student council president! For goodness' sake, she is already president of . . . of . . . Socktopia! Isn't that enough?"

Fara knew not to correct her. She looked at Mr. Z. The room was quiet. Even the walls seemed to be holding their breath.

"Well," said Mr. Z. finally, "no. As I told Fara initially, it doesn't matter how the publicity came to pass, she still skirted the rules and was flirting with trouble."

Fara was ashamed to hear this again, especially in front of Melodee, her mother, and the principal. But she realized with some surprise that she wasn't very disappointed. It would have been great to be named president, but after hearing the whole story, she only cared that Melodee wasn't. And that Ms. Simon wasn't First Mom.

"All right," said Mr. Cluver after some time. "I agree with Mr. Zolitski. Neither of you girls will be president. Mr.

Zolitski and I will address the issue of finding a new student council president later. To be honest," he muttered to Mr. Z., "something like this makes me want to get rid of student council altogether."

Ms. Simon leaned over Mr. Cluver's desk. "This isn't over," she said.

Mr. Cluver laughed. "Oh, that's for sure," he said. "Fara, Melodee, thank you for your time. Mr. Zolitski, you'd better get to your class; we'll talk later. Ms. Simon," he said with a hint of a smile, "sit down. You are going to be here for a while."

30. A President Who Doesn't Sock

THE RED FOX READER

The Official Newspaper of

Stockville Middle School

STUDENT COUNCIL PRESIDENT REMOVED

AFTER LESS THAN ONE WEEK IN OFFICE

by Jody Gower

Believe it or not, political scandal has reached a new low—low age, that is. Eleven-year-old Melodee Simon was removed from the office of sixth-grade student council president after admitting that her mother helped get candidate Fara Ross disqualified. In a meeting with Principal Cluver and student council adviser Mr. Zolitski, Melodee's mother, Ms. Linda Simon, admitted to telling WSTV about an event involving Ross when she knew that outside publicity would get Ross in trouble.

Mr. Cluver decided that neither Melodee Simon nor Fara Ross is allowed to be student council president. In a recent interview, Mr. Zolitski explained, "We are trying to have fair elections and an honest student government. I am extremely disappointed that neither candidate played by the rules. That's politics, but we won't stand for it here. If only our country wouldn't stand for it either."

Vice president and soccer team assistant captain Neil Harrow said, "I'm glad that Mr. Z. didn't let Melodee stay president. What her mom did was really low." Secretary Tania Farucci agreed. "I can't believe [Melodee] wanted to win that badly. I mean, what's the big deal?"

Also, Ms. Linda Simon resigned from her position of president of the Stockville Middle School Parent-Teacher Association (PTA). This is the first time in seven years that Ms. Simon is not president of the PTA. She started as president of the Harvey Elementary School PTA when her daughter was in kindergarten.

There is no new PTA president yet.

There is also no new student council president yet. Mr. Zolitski announced that anyone who wants to run should hand in an essay to him by Friday. Since they want to get a president quickly, there will not be as much campaigning as there was in the first election, so helping a candidate will not be worth extra credit in social studies.

Vicki threw her copy of the school newspaper on the table. "Cool," she said. "Good article."

"Really?" asked Jody, her eyes lighting up.

"Yes," said Caroline, who put down her copy and picked up her sandwich.

"Good front-page material," Fara agreed.

"What do you think, Phillip?" asked Jody.

"Huh?" Phillip looked up from his copy of the newspaper, which was open to an article about the addition of salami to the cafeteria's lunch meat selections.

"Wasn't Jody's article good?" prompted Fara.

"Oh, yeah. The whole paper's good. Did you see that the flute ensemble played at a nursing home last weekend?"

Caroline giggled. Vicki rolled her eyes.

"But your article is extra good," Phillip said quickly.

"I agree," said Fara.

Vicki rolled her eyes again. Things between her and Fara weren't completely back to normal yet. Fara had apologized, but it took Vicki a long time to accept apologies. After Caroline told her that it took Vicki more than two weeks to forgive Daniella French for borrowing a CD and losing it, Fara was happy that Vicki would even permit her and her orange and argyle socks to sit with them at lunch again.

"Can I tell them the juicy part?" Jody asked Fara.

"You mean that Melodee and Zoë are cousins?" said Vicki. "Old news."

"No, the even juicier juicy part," said Jody.

"Tell us!" said Caroline, her face glowing to match her pink shirt.

"When I was interviewing soccer-player-Neil for the article," Jody said, "he told me that he was hoping they'd make Fara president because then he'd get to have meetings with her every week! So I gave him her phone number!"

Everyone oohed, and it was Fara's turn to become pink.

"He wanted to work *closely* with her," Jody sang.

"I bet he's glad to not have to work closely with Melodee," said Vicki.

"I bet Melodee wasn't really sick when she stayed home on Monday," said Phillip.

Fara was grateful for the change of subject. "Well," she

said, "you can't really blame her. It would have been suicide to come into school after what happened." As angry as she was, Fara had been able to relate to Melodee's empty desk in homeroom that day. She had even wished—for a very, very short moment—that her own mother had been like Ms. Simon and let her stay home.

"I heard that Melodee might leave and go to private school for the rest of the year," said Jody. "But I couldn't write that because I didn't know if it was true. I don't want people to think of the *Red Fox Reader* as a tabloid."

"You should start a school tabloid just so *that* news could go on the front page," said Vicki.

"A school tabloid?" said Jody, nose crinkled. "I strive for excellence in reporting."

Phillip opened a bag of fruit snacks and pointed to Jody's article. "Who do you think is going to run for president now?" he asked.

Vicki cleared her throat loudly.

"You?" Jody asked. Fara could tell she was already brainstorming headlines.

"No," said Vicki. "Not me."

Caroline put down her sandwich and smiled sheepishly.

"You?" said Phillip.

"Really?" asked Fara.

Caroline shrugged. "I think so," she said quietly. Then

she straightened and looked everyone in the eye. "Well, yes," she said.

Vicki grinned and patted Caroline on the back.

"I really thought a lot of your ideas were worthwhile," Caroline said to Fara. "Especially the recycling one. We throw away so much paper. I have a few ideas of my own, too, of course. But we can talk about that at our campaign team meeting." She looked around the table. "That is, I hope you'll all be my campaign team."

"I'd be honored!"

"Yeah, me too."

"Duh."

"If Mr. Z. lets me."

Only Caroline's cheeks turned pink, and only slightly. "Good!" she said. "I already put in my application, and I actually asked Mr. Z. if you could be on my team—if that's all right, Fara."

"Oh, yeah." Fara was impressed. Caroline had really thought this through. "What did he say?"

Vicki answered, her eyes slightly untrusting. "He thought about it for a while, but then he finally said you could as long as you aren't her campaign manager—but I'm it anyway. And you won't get extra credit in social studies for it—but no one will anyway."

Fara nodded. "That sounds fair."

"Okay," said Caroline quietly. She swallowed the last bite of her turkey sandwich and wiped her mouth with her napkin. "Well then, since the whole team is here, why don't we have our first meeting right now? We've got a lot to do before the election, and it's only next week."

Fara smiled. Caroline wasn't a loud leader, but that didn't mean she wouldn't be a good one. "Sounds good to me," she said.

"Yeah, Caroline!" said Phillip. "What should your slogan be?"

"Caroline Will Be Fine," said Vicki as though it should have been obvious.

"But she'll be more than fine," said Jody. "Caroline Ma Will Be a Great President-a!" she suggested.

"Caroline Ma Is Spectaculah!" said Fara.

"How about Caroline Ma Will Care for Ya?" said Vicki.

Phillip gasped and almost choked on his milk. "That's good," he said.

"Well, we want her to win," said Fara, "so her slogan should be something that shows she's not Melodee *or* me."

Jody started to laugh.

"What?" asked Vicki.

Jody shook her head. "Nothing," she said. Then she started to laugh harder.

"Tell us," said Phillip.

Jody grinned. "Caroline Doesn't Sock."

31. Team Ma

WITH ALL OF THE EXCITEMENT AND SCANDAL
surrounding student council, more people decided to run
the second time. Caroline faced two tough competitors.
The first was Diana Klein, the secretary's best friend, whose
posters featured the words "Vote Diana for an Awesome
Year" around a glamorous picture of her in her cheerleading
uniform. The second was a boy named Trent Loren, who,
rather than hanging posters, spread word of his candidacy by
having members of his campaign team circulate notes that
said "Vote for Trent" in all of their classes. They got caught
so many times throughout the week that Trent was able to
secure the votes of everyone in detention.

With such popular opponents, Caroline asked everyone to help her make her quiet voice heard. Phillip was to
design her posters, which would say "SMS Will Shine with

Caroline!" and then everyone would help color them in and hang them up. She asked Fara for feedback on her ideas and Jody for input on her speech. And Vicki, who was prouder of Caroline than anyone, even Caroline's parents, kept everyone on task and full of candy. Under Caroline's unassuming but efficient leadership, Team Ma operated like a well-oiled presidential machine.

Fara could not have been more impressed with how responsible and serious Caroline was about running for president. In addition to her posters she photocopied flyers with a list of her main ideas, all of which Fara found to be intelligent and practical. Besides starting a recycling club, Caroline wanted to start a fund-raising committee right away to hold monthly bake sales to raise money for the sixth-grade dance. Her best idea, though, Fara thought, was to start a program that would pair new middle schoolers with soon-to-be eighth graders as buddies who would show them around at orientation. That way new sixth graders would learn their way around middle school from insiders, and they would have an automatic older friend when they arrived in September.

"Phillip helped me come up with that idea," Caroline told her team while they were handing out the flyers after school the day before the election.

"Vote for Caroline!" shouted Vicki. She handed flyers to some passing students.

"Well," said Phillip, blushing, "I just told her that I had to ask an eighth grader for directions to the bathroom on the first day. Caroline thought of the rest."

"SMS Will Shine with Caroline!" shouted Vicki. She made a flyer into a paper airplane and launched it after a group of students.

"If there are middle school buddies," Jody said excitedly, "we could do a feature in the *Red Fox Reader* every month that interviews a sixth grader and their buddy. It could be called the Companion Corner. Or wait, I've got it, Buddy Beat!"

"It's probably not too late to even start the buddy thing for this year," Fara said to Caroline. "I really hope you win."

Caroline smiled and shrugged. "Me too," she confessed. "But even if I don't, I think I'll try to get the buddy thing going anyway."

Fara grinned back at her. Now *that* was the way to make a difference. No waiting for a position of influence, no hesitating and second-guessing the timing; just recognizing a problem and setting about fixing it. Flexing her toes in her mauve sock and indigo sock, Fara realized that that's what she had done with the Sockinental Congress—she'd worked to make a difference even though there were obstacles in her way. And that was pretty successful . . . before it exploded and demolished everything in its wake, at least. She sighed.

Melodee and her mother might have lit the fuse, but Fara knew she—she alone—had planted the dynamite. Glancing around at her friends, who were shamelessly showcasing their support for Caroline, Fara felt profoundly grateful for the chance to rebuild.

She grabbed a stack of flyers and began to pass them out to everyone who passed. "Vote for Caroline!" she shouted.

32. Blank

FARA GLANCED AT HER CLOCK: 11:30. SHE'D been lying in bed for almost two hours, yet she just couldn't fall asleep. Her mind was swimming with thoughts of Caroline and individuality and freedom and socks. She'd flipped over her pillow so many times that neither side was cold anymore. She even tried counting sheep, but she stopped when she kept envisioning sheep wearing socks. Finally she flicked on her light and took out her journal and a pencil.

"I really, really, really, REALLY hope that Caroline wins," Fara scribbled quickly. Then she thought, with a frown of embarrassment, *I really, really wish that I had won.* "I can still make a difference without being president," Fara wrote. "Right?" She scribbled it out. "Just like Caroline will do the buddy thing if she doesn't win." She paused. "But it'd be so much easier if I was."

She stared across the room at her sock drawers. If she had won the election, she wouldn't have to rely on socks anymore. But what was she relying on them for now? She didn't really want fame, and she had already made her statement. She wanted a new one.

"Fara Ross, Sock Girl," she wrote in her journal. Then she skipped a line and wrote, "Fara Ross, _____."

With a sigh, Fara closed her journal and turned off the light. She'd been craving freedom of footwear, but now that she could have it, she was almost afraid to exercise it. She wasn't quite ready to be a blank.

33. Election Day

THE NEXT MORNING THE TEAM GATHERED
around Caroline at her locker before homeroom. She was
wearing a gray pencil skirt and a pink sweater that comple-
mented her pink cheeks. She was even quieter than usual,
just leaning against her locker and smoothing her sweater
while Vicki paced to the water fountain and back.

"Do you have your speech?" Vicki asked. "I've got an extra
copy in case you don't."

"I've got it," Caroline said.

"Okay, well, I'll follow along on my copy from the front row,
and if you lose your place, or if you're missing a page or something, just look at me and I'll tell you what comes next."

Caroline giggled and nodded.

"Remember," said Jody, "you're the best person for the
job."

"Yeah," said Fara. "What you have to say is ten million times better than what Diana and Trent have to say, combined."

"Remember to tell them good luck," said Vicki, "but you can have your fingers crossed when you do."

"Behind your back, of course," said Jody.

"Don't knock over the podium," advised Phillip with a knowing look.

"And don't be nervous," said Vicki as she bit her nails.

"And also don't forget to smile," said Jody. "Since your slogan has to do with shining."

"And whatever you do," added Fara, "don't talk about socks."

When Fara walked into the auditorium with the rest of the sixth grade at the start of first period and saw Diana, Trent, and Caroline sitting on the stage, she couldn't help but feel a pang of jealousy. Images of the blank line beside her name flashed into her head. She wanted to be up there, waiting anxiously to deliver her carefully planned speech. She wanted to stir the audience with her eloquent words and novel ideas. Caroline would make a great president—Fara knew that for sure—but she wondered if anyone else would be able to tell, or if they'd even pay attention to a small, sweet girl with a soft voice and matching white socks.

Someone grabbed her hand and whisked her toward a row in the middle of the auditorium. It was Jody, and her other hand was pushing Phillip along into the row. "We have to send Caroline good-luck vibes," said Jody. "Goodluckgoodluckgoodluck," she chanted.

"Good luck," chanted Phillip. He stuck out his arms and wiggled his fingers just as a girl sat down in the seat in front, and he ended up tickling her on the neck. She spun around and gave him a poisonous look. "Whoops, sorry," said Phillip. "Um, vote for Caroline."

"Yeah, and pass it on," said Fara. She wiggled her fingers.

The girl looked at her for a few seconds like she was crazy, but then she laughed, tickled the girl next to her, and said, "Vote for Caroline, pass it on."

The three of them tried not to laugh as they watched the tickle and the message continue down the row. But when it reached some boys toward the aisle, it turned into a poke, and then a push, and then a wet willy. "Vote for Caroline," laughed a boy as he stuck his wet finger into the next boy's ear. "Pass it on!"

Mr. Z. stepped up to the microphone and tapped on it to get everyone's attention. "Welcome, once again, to the sixth-grade student council elections. This will work much the same as it did last time. We have three lovely candidates for you to listen to. They will read their speeches in alphabetical order. Then your teachers will pass around ballots, and you will mark the *one* candidate you think would make the best student council president. Marking two people cancels out your vote, and writing someone in, such as Batman"— someone, probably the person who wrote in Batman during the first election, cheered—"also cancels out your vote, since Batman, or anyone but these three, isn't in the running. So to cut right to the action, here is your first candidate, Miss Diana Klein."

Diana walked to the podium and adjusted the microphone. She cleared her throat and the room filled with screechy feedback. "For those of you who don't know me," she began, "my name is Diana Klein and I am running for student council president." Fara listened as Diana spoke about suggestion boxes and school spirit, much the way Melodee had when it was her turn. She said that if she was elected, anyone could come up to her in the hallway and give her a suggestion and she would listen to it. But that was about it. "In conclusion," Diana said, "vote for me, Diana Klein, for an awesome year. Thank you."

Fara applauded politely with everyone else.

"She's got *nothing* on Caroline," whispered Phillip.

Mr. Z. went to the podium again. "Thank you, Diana. Next is Trent Loren. Trent?"

Trent, who was wearing jeans with tears in them and a T-shirt that looked wrinkly even from Fara's faraway seat, walked confidently up to the podium and shook Mr. Z.'s hand. "Hey, what's up," he said. "For those of you who don't know me, I'm Trent, and I'm also running for president." In the time it took Fara to wonder why so many people started their speeches with "For those of you who don't know me . . . ," Trent's speech was over. "So in conclusion," Trent said, "I don't want to make you promises I can't keep. So I'm not going to make you any promises. Vote for Trent, the honest candidate, for president."

"What was that?" Jody whispered to Fara. "He just got up there and promised he'd do absolutely nothing if he wins!"

"Really?" said Phillip. "That's really what he said? I thought I missed something."

But the cheers for "the honest candidate" were raucous, louder by far than the ones for Diana. Fara sighed loudly and shifted so that her right leg was curled under her. *Come on, Caroline,* she thought. *Knock their socks off.*

Mr. Z. walked to the podium. "Okay, Trent," he said in such a way that made Fara think he couldn't really believe Trent's platform either. "Last up is Caroline Ma."

Fara, Jody, and Phillip applauded as loudly as they could as Caroline stood, approached the podium, and straightened out her skirt.

"Do you know her?" Fara heard someone behind her whisper.

"I think she's friends with that sock girl," the other whispered back.

The crowd quieted down, but Caroline just stood there staring out at everyone. After about three seconds of silence Fara worried that maybe Caroline had actually started but was speaking so softly no one could hear. Luckily, her gentle voice started coming through the speakers clearly.

"My first day at Stockville Middle School," Caroline said, "I went up to the second floor and made a left to try to find room 202. I ended up walking around the whole floor before I found it . . . just to the *right* of the staircase." Phillip laughed loudly, and Fara thought she heard a few other twitters in the crowd. She smiled and waved her fingers at her sides to send Caroline some good vibes. "Yes, we had orientation in June," Caroline said, "and it was helpful, but it still took a little bit of time to get to know the school. Actually, I'm still not *completely* sure where some things are or how some things work," she said shyly. Fara saw her face turn red. She crossed her fingers. "That's why if I, Caroline Ma, am elected, I will start a program that teams up eighth graders with new sixth graders to show them around the school during orientation and the beginning of the year." Fara had to keep herself from breaking into applause right then, and from the way Jody was biting her lip and Phillip was sitting on his hands, she guessed they felt the same way. She glanced around the room. People seemed to be paying attention. Caroline continued her speech, describing the buddies program, the fund-raising committee for the dance, and her desire to make Stockville Middle School an even better place. She finished with her motto, "SMS Will Shine with Caroline. Thank you for your time. And good luck to Trent Loren and Diana Klein." Caroline covered her mouth. "I didn't mean for that to rhyme," she said. Everyone laughed. Caroline, tomato red, opened her mouth but then closed it again and went back to her seat.

Fara, Jody, and Phillip jumped up and applauded until their hands hurt. Fara could see Vicki standing in the front row as well. Caroline was beaming on the stage, and she motioned slightly for Vicki to sit down.

"She was fantastic!" Jody gushed.

"That rhyming part at the end was really funny," Phillip said.

"Let's just hope everyone agrees," Fara said, still applauding.

Teachers came down the aisles and passed out ballot sheets. The three of them marked theirs quickly and folded them up. "Who are you voting for?" the girl behind Fara asked her neighbor.

"Eh, probably Trent," he responded.

Trent! How could anyone who just heard the speeches vote for *Trent*? And the way he'd said it, as though he wasn't even going to consider the options . . . how was anyone supposed to make a difference when no one else cared? Fara wanted to spin around and rip up their ballots, just to make a statement.

When the students started filing out, the three of them pushed their way to the front to congratulate Caroline. "Well, I did my best," Caroline said softly.

"Anyone who doesn't vote for you is stupid," Vicki said. She crossed her arms.

Caroline just smiled and shrugged.

Tania and the other officers were around Diana, congratulating her and surveying the crowd, but soccer-player-Neil broke away and tapped Fara on the shoulder. "Hi," he said.

"Oh, hi."

"It, um, sucks that you had to drop out."

Fara grinned. He didn't say "it socks." "Nah," she said. "I voted for Caroline."

Neil glanced at Diana and lowered his voice. "I did too." He smiled.

34. Making a Statement

WHEN THE ANNOUNCEMENT CAME AT THE
end of eighth period that the new sixth-grade president was
Caroline Ma, Fara was so thrilled she jumped out of her
seat. She was so happy about everything—that the news
had come so quickly, that her friend had done it, that the
student council president would actually do something
for the good of the school, that her classmates had cared
enough to vote for the person with the best ideas, and that
she had friends to celebrate with. That was all something,
wasn't it?

Caroline wanted to get right to work. "I'm going to set up a
recycling club as soon as I can," she told Fara after school. "Do
you want to be president of it? It was your idea to begin with."

Fara bubbled with excitement. *Fara Ross, Recycling Club
President,* she thought. But something about it didn't seem

right. "That's okay," she said. "I think you'll do a great job with it."

Caroline turned bright red. "Are you sure?" she asked. "Of course I'll give you credit for it, though."

Fara shrugged. She wiggled her toes in her blue sock and zigzagged sock and realized that she didn't even want the credit; she had had enough exposure and excitement to last her a long time—well, at least until Thanksgiving. *The important thing is that the difference be made,* she thought, *even if I'm not the one to make it.*

As she wrote that very thought in her journal that afternoon, she realized that she wasn't writing it to try and convince herself, but because she was already convinced. Maybe that was the statement she'd been looking to make. It was quiet, but that didn't mean it couldn't do good things. *Like Caroline,* she thought.

She flipped back to the page from the night before. She erased the blank line. Now beneath "Fara Ross, Sock Girl" it just said "Fara Ross."

"That's better," she said aloud.

Fara got up and looked at the mush of colors in her sock drawers. She slipped off her blue sock and zigzagged sock and added them to the pile. Picking through the drawers, she found the socks she was looking for and put them on her feet: white and white.

Then she emptied the contents of her sock drawers into two plastic bags and carried them downstairs to the closet with the rest of the donations for the clothing drive.

"What're you doing, Far?" her parents asked her on her way back.

Fara grinned. "Re-sock-ling," she said.